訓練聽力　增加字彙

　　英語聽力是學習英語的重要一環，必須提早開始，長期訓練。而且要有計劃地反覆練習，絕不能只學聽單自認圖片，一定要聽句子，而且要逐漸拉長句子的內容，才能學習到英語的真諦。

　　本書分為〔上〕、〔中〕、〔下〕引導學生在學習上循序漸進，逐步加強，期望能在12年國教國中會考考試中，一舉拿下聽力的滿分。本書的另一特色為在快樂學習中增加單字的記憶和使用能力，透過反覆的聽力測驗，不但大量增加字彙的累積，在不知不覺中也學會了說與寫的能力，可謂一舉數得，而且輕鬆易得。

　　為減輕學生的聽力障礙，本書將考題敘述的每個句子及答案，都精心譯為中文，以供學生參考。

1. 隨時注意 7 個 W：who, when, what, where, which, why, how
　　　　也就是人、時、事、地、物、原因、狀態

2. 能夠與不能 (ability and inability)
　　　　常用字詞有：can, be able to, could, can't, couldn't, not be able to, neither

　1)　　A: How many languages can you speak?
　　　　B: I can/am able to speak three languages fluently.
　　　　翻譯：A：你能說幾種語言？
　　　　　　　　B：我能流利的說三種語言。

　2)　　A: Has he bought a new house?
　　　　B: No. He's never been able to save money.
　　　　翻譯：A：他買新房子了嗎？
　　　　　　　　B：不，他永遠沒有能力存錢。

　3)　　A: I couldn't do the homework. It was too difficult.
　　　　B: Neither could I.
　　　　翻譯：A：我不會做作業。太難了。
　　　　　　　　B：我也不會。

3. 勸告與建議 (advice and suggestion)
　　　　常用字詞有：had better, I think, let's, OK, yes, good idea, sure, why not,

1) A: I've got a headache today.

   B: You'd better go to see the doctor./I think you should go to see the
   doctor.

   翻譯：A：我今天頭痛。

          B：你最好去看醫生。我想你應該去看醫生。

2) A: I've got a terrible stomachache.

   B: You'd better not go on working.

   A: OK./All right./Thank you for your advice.

   翻譯：A：我的胃痛死了。

          B：你最好不要上班。

          C：好的/沒問題/謝謝你的勸告。

3) A: Let's go, shall we?

   B: Yes, let's./I'm afraid it's too early.

   翻譯：A：我們走吧，要不要？

          B：好，走吧。/我怕太晚了。

4) A: What/How about going fishing now?

   B: That's a good idea./That sounds interesting./Sure. Why not?

   翻譯：A：現在去釣魚怎麼樣？

          B：好主意。/聽起來很有趣。/當然，有何不可？

5) A: Let's go to the concert.

   B: I don't feel like it. Why don't we go to the beach instead?

   翻譯：A：我們去聽音樂會吧。

          B：我不想去。我們為什麼不去海邊？

4. 同意與不同意（agreement and disagreement）

常用字詞有：I think so. I hope so. I don't think so. I agree. I don't agree. So can I. Me too. Neither can I. I can't, either.

1) A: The book is interesting.

   B: I think so, too.

   翻譯：A：這本書很有趣。

          B：我也這麼想。

2) A: Do you think people will be able to live on the moon in the future?

B: I hope so, but I don't think so.

翻譯：A：你認為人類將來能住到月球上嗎？

B：希望如此，但我不認為能夠。

3) A: This lesson is interesting, isn't it?

B: I don't think so./I'm afraid I can't agree with you./I'm afraid I don't quite agree with you./I'm afraid it isn't.

翻譯：A：這堂課很有趣，不是嗎？

B：我不這樣認為。恐怕我無法同意你。我恐怕不十分同意你。恐怕不是這樣。

4) A: I can swim well.

B: So can I./Me too.

翻譯：A：我很會游泳。

B：我也是。

5) A: I can't play the guitar.

B: Neither can I./I can't, either.

翻譯：A：我不會彈吉他。

B：我也不會。

5. 道歉（Apology）

常用字詞有：Sorry. I'm sorry about ….

A: Sorry./I'm terribly sorry about that.

B: That's all right./Never mind./Don't worry.

翻譯：A：抱歉。關於那件事我非常抱歉。

B：沒關係。不要放在心上。不要擔心。

6. 讚賞（Appreciation）

常用字詞有：That's a good idea. That sounds interesting. Fantastic! Amazing! Well done ! That's wonderful.

1) A: I've got the first prize.

B: Well done ! /You deserved to win./That's wonderful news.

翻譯：A：我得第一名。

B：真棒。你實至名歸。真是個棒消息。

2) A: We had a surprise birthday party on Saturday afternoon.

B: That was a super afternoon.

翻譯：A：星期六下午的生日聚會令人驚喜。

　　　　B：那是個超棒的下午。

3)　　A: He broke the world record for the two mile run.

　　　　B: Fantastic!/Amazing!

翻譯：A：他在兩英哩賽跑打破世界紀錄。

　　　　B：了不起。又驚又喜。

7. 肯定與不肯定 (certainty and uncertainty)

常用字詞有：sure, not sure, perhaps, maybe, possible, possibly,

1)　　A: Are you sure?

　　　　B: Yes, I am./No, I'm not.

翻譯：A：你確定嗎？

　　　　B：是的，我確定。不，我不確定。

2)　　A: When will Mary go to school?

　　　　B: Perhaps/Maybe she'll go at eight.

翻譯：A：Mary 何時上學？

　　　　B：或許 8 歲。

3)　　A: His ambition is to be an architect.

　　　　B: He'll possibly go to university after he leaves school.

翻譯：A：他的願望是當建築師。

　　　　B：他離開學校後可能要念大學。

8. 比較 (Comparison)

常用字詞有：as...as..., not so... as..., more... than..., less...than...,

1)　　A: How tall is Sue?

　　　　B: 1.6 meters. She's not so tall as Jane.

　　　　A: What about Mary?

　　　　B: She's as tall as Sue.

翻譯：A：Sue 身高多少。

　　　　B：160 公分。她不像 Jane 那麼高。

　　　　A：那 Mary 呢？

B：她跟 Sue 一樣高。

2)　A: Which is more important, electricity or water?

B: It's hard to say.

翻譯：A：哪個比較重要，水還是電？

　　　　B：很難說。

9. 關心 (Concern)

常用字詞有：Is anything wrong? What's the matter? What's wrong with ....? What's the matter with ....? How's ......?

1)　A: What's wrong with you?/What's the matter with you?

B: I've got a cold.

翻譯：A：你怎麼了？

　　　　B：我感冒了。

2)　A: How's your mother?

B: She's worse than yesterday.

A: I'm sorry to hear that. Don't worry too much. She'll get better soon.

翻譯：A：令堂狀況如何。

　　　　B：她比昨天更糟了。

　　　　A：我聽了很遺憾。不用太擔心。她很快就會好一些。

4)　A: What's the matter?

B: I can't find my car key.

翻譯：A：發生甚麼事？

　　　　B：我找不到汽車鑰匙。

10. 詢問 (Inquiries)

常用字詞有：How, when, where, who, why, what

1)　A: Excuse me, how can I get to the railway station?

B: Take a No. 41 bus.

翻譯：A：對不起，要如何到火車站去？

　　　　B：搭 41 號公車。

2)　A: Excuse me. When does the next train leave for Kaohsuing?

B: 10 a.m.

翻譯：A：對不起。去高雄的下一班火車是甚麼時候？
B：上午十點。

3) A: What's the weather like today?
B: It'll rain this afternoon.
翻譯：A：今天天氣如何？
B：下午會下雨。

4) A: How far is your home from the school?
B: Five minutes by bike.
翻譯：A：你家距離學校有多遠？
B：騎單車5分鐘。

11. 意向 (Intentions)

常用字詞有：I'd like ..., Would you like to...? What do you want ...?

1) A: What do you want to be in the future?
B: I want to be a businessman.
翻譯：A：你將來想當甚麼？
B：我想當生意人。

2) A: Would you like to work at the South Pole in the future?
B: Yes, we'd love to.
翻譯：A：你將來喜歡在南極工作嗎？
B：是的，我會喜歡。

3) A: I'd like fried eggs with peas and pork, too.
B: OK.
翻譯：A：我想要豆子、豬肉炒蛋。
B：沒問題。

12. 喜歡、不喜歡/偏愛 (Likes, dislikes and preferences)

常用字詞有：like, dislike, prefer, enjoy

1) A: Which kind of apples do you prefer, red ones or green ones?
   B: Green ones.
   翻譯：A：你比較喜歡哪一種蘋果，紅的還是綠的？
   　　　B：綠的。

2) A: Do you enjoy music or dance?
   B: I enjoy music.
   翻譯：A：你喜歡音樂還是跳舞？
   　　　B：我喜歡音樂。

3) A: How did you like the play?
   B: It was wonderful.
   翻譯：A：這齣戲你覺得如何？
   　　　B：很棒。

13. 提供 (Offers)

常用字詞有：Can I ....? Let me .... What can I ...? Would you like ...?

1) A: Can I help you?
   B: Yes, please.
   翻譯：A：可以幫你忙嗎？
   　　　B：是的，謝謝。

2) A: Let me help you.
   B: Thanks.
   翻譯：A：我來幫你忙。
   　　　B：謝謝。

3) A: Would you like a drink?
   B: That's very kind of you.
   翻譯：A：要來杯飲料嗎？
   　　　B：你真好意。

4) A: Shall I get a trolley for you?
   B: No, thanks.
   翻譯：A：要我拿輛手推車給你嗎？
   　　　B：不用，謝謝。

全新國中會考英語聽力精選 中冊
目　　錄

測驗題

全文翻譯

全新國中會考英語聽力精選(中)

Unit 1

Ⅰ、Listen and choose the right picture.（根據你所聽到的內容，選出相應的圖片。）（6分）

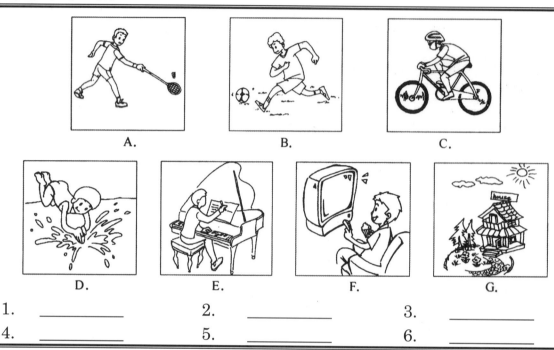

A.　　　　　　B.　　　　　　C.

D.　　　E.　　　F.　　　G.

1. _____　　2. _____　　3. _____

4. _____　　5. _____　　6. _____

Ⅱ、Listen to the dialogue and choose the best answer to the question you hear.（根據你所聽到的對話和問題，選出最恰當的答案。）（10分）

（　）7. (A)John's family is bigger.　　(B)John's family is smaller.
　　　　 (C)Kate's family is bigger.　　(D)Kate's family is smaller.

（　）8. (A)Yes, I am.　　(B)Yes, she is.　　(C)No, I'm not.　　(D)No, she isn't.

（　）9. (A)Football.　　(B)Swimming.　　(C)Tennis.　　(D)Table tennis.

（　）10. (A)They are in a clothes shop.　　(B)They are at the fruit stall.
　　　　 (C)They are in the cinema.　　(D)They are at the hospital.

（　）11. (A)He was travelling there.
　　　　 (B)He had a meeting there.
　　　　 (C)He went to meet the woman there.
　　　　 (D)He visited some relatives there.

（　）12. (A)Yes, he will.　　(B)No, he won't.
　　　　 (C)Yes, he did.　　(D)No, he didn't.

（　）13. (A)He advised her to take her raincoat with her.
　　　　(B)He advised her to take her umbrella with her.
　　　　(C)He advised her not to take her umbrella with her.
　　　　(D)He advised her not to take her raincoat with her.

（　）14. (A)Noise pollution.　　　　　　(B)Air pollution.
　　　　(C)Water pollution.　　　　　　(D)Land pollution.

（　）15. (A)At the boy's flat.　　　　　　(B)At the girl's flat.
　　　　(C)At the cinema.　　　　　　　(D)At his own home.

（　）16. (A)Brother and sister.　　　　　(B)Father and daughter.
　　　　(C)Son and mother.　　　　　　(D)Workmates.

Ⅲ、**Listen to the letter and decide whether the following statements are True (T) or False (F).**（判斷下列句子是否符合你所聽到的信件的內容，符合的用 T 表示，不符合的用 F 表示。）（7分）

（　）17. Kitty receives a letter from Kelly.

（　）18. Sally, who stands on the right of Kitty, is from the UK.

（　）19. Kelly usually plays table tennis with Alice at school.

（　）20. Danny can draw very well.

（　）21. Peter practises playing tennis every day.

（　）22. Bill is quite good at sports.

（　）23. Kitty wants to know something about Kelly's friends.

Ⅳ、**Listen to the passage and fill in the blanks.**（根據你聽到的短文，完成下列內容，每空格限填一詞。）（7分）

● Jane is __24__ years old.

● Jane is __25__ centimetres tall.

● Jane has __26__ hair.

● Jane speaks English and she can speak a little __27__.

● Jane's parents work as __28__.

● Jane's sister, Helen is an __29__.

● Jane is __30__ the floor in the classroom.

24. _____　　25. _____　　26. _____　　27. _____
28. _____　　29. _____　　30. _____

全新國中會考英語聽力精選(中)

Unit 2

Ⅰ、Listen and choose the right picture.（根據你所聽到的內容,選出相應的圖片。）（6分）

A

B

C

D

E

F

G

1. _____   2. _____   3. _____
4. _____   5. _____   6. _____

Ⅱ、Listen and choose the best response to the sentence you hear.（根據你所聽到的句子,選出最恰當的應答句。）（6分）

( ) 7.　(A)Yes, I will.　　　　　　　(B)No, I won't.
　　　　(C)Yes, I won't.　　　　　　(D)No, I will.

( ) 8.　(A)At three in the morning.　(B)In Shanghai.
　　　　(C)With my parents.　　　　 (D)Taiwan.

( ) 9.　(A)Germany.　　　　　　　　(B)China.
　　　　(C)American.　　　　　　　 (D)Australia.

( ) 10.　(A)So do I.　　　　　　　　(B)Neither do I.
　　　　 (C)So have I.　　　　　　　(D)Neither haven't I.

( ) 11.　(A)That's a good idea.　　　 (B)I'm afraid you are wrong.
　　　　 (C)That's all right.　　　　　(D)You are welcome.

( ) 12.　(A)Here is it.　　　　　　　 (B)Here you are.
　　　　 (C)It is here.　　　　　　　 (D)No, I don't.

( ) 13. (A)German.   (B)American.
       (C)English.   (D)French.

( ) 14. (A)The teachers' office.   (B)On the third floor.
       (C)The library.   (D)The lab.

( ) 15. (A)This Saturday.   (B)This Sunday morning.
       (C)At the airport.   (D)At home.

( ) 16. (A)45.   (B)15.
       (C)30.   (D)35.

( ) 17. (A)At a hotel.   (B)At a clinic.
       (C)In a supermarket.   (D)In a shopping mall.

( ) 18. (A)1.   (B)2.
       (C)3.   (D)4.

Ⅳ、Listen to the dialogue and decide whether the following statements are True (T) or False (F).（判斷下列句子內容是否符合你所聽到的對話內容,符合的用"T"表示,不符合的用"F"表示。）（6分）

( ) 19. Danny is an Australian.

( ) 20. One of his favorite interests is playing the guitar.

( ) 21. His job is to draw plans of buildings.

( ) 22. Danny has to work over 8 hours every day.

( ) 23. He never takes work home.

( ) 24. We keep in touch with each other twice a month.

Ⅴ、Listen and fill in the blanks.（根據你所聽到的內容,用適當的單詞完成下面的句子。每空格限填一詞。）（6分）

25. The man was going to fly to _____.

26. The man wanted the flight on the date of _____.

27. The number of the flight was _____.

28. The flight was at Gate _____ , New York City Airport.

29. The departure time of the flight was at _____.

30. The man paid _____ for the ticket.

Unit 3

Ⅰ、Listen and choose the right picture.（根據你所聽到的內容，選出相應的圖片。）（6分）

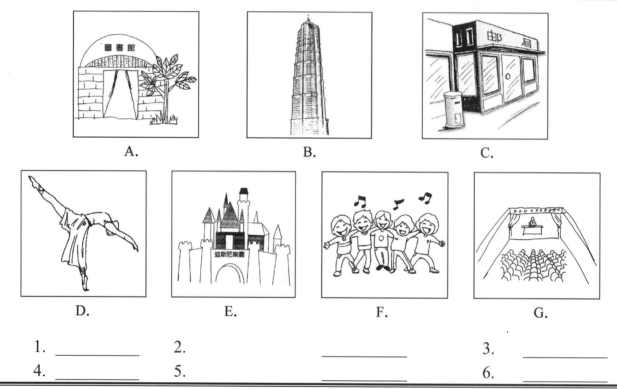

A.   B.   C.

D.   E.   F.   G.

1. _____   2. _____   3. _____
4. _____   5. _____   6. _____

Ⅱ、Listen and choose the best response to the sentence you hear.（根據你所聽到的句子，選出最恰當的應答句。）（6分）

(   ) 7.   (A)He is handsome.   (B)He is watering the flowers.
       (C)He likes reading.   (D)He is kind and friendly.

(   ) 8.   (A)That's right.   (B)I'm right.
       (C)All right.   (D)That's all right.

(   ) 9.   (A)To wash clothes.   (B)To wash dishes.
       (C)To clean houses.   (D)To make the air clean.

(   ) 10.   (A)I thinks so.   (B)No, I don't think so.
       (C)I hope not.   (D)I hope so.

(   ) 11.   (A)So was I.   (B)Neither was I.
       (C)So do I.   (D)Neither do I.

(   ) 12.   (A)Are you kidding?   (B)No, of course not."
       (C)Thank you.   (D)Congratulations.

( ) 13. (A)She is beautiful.   (B)She is kind.
     (C)She loses her temper easily.   (D)She never scolds her son.

( ) 14. (A)210 pages.   (B)4 pages.
     (C)240 pages.   (D)120 pages.

( ) 15. (A)Jerry.   (B)Tom.   (C)Sam.   (D)Jim.

( ) 16. (A)Rainy.   (B)Sunny.   (C)Hot.   (D)Windy.

( ) 17. (A)7.30.   (B)7.15.   (C)7.10.   (D)7.20.

( ) 18. (A)In the office.   (B)In a hospital.
     (C)At a bus stop.   (D)In a supermarket.

Ⅳ、Listen to the passage and decide whether the following statements are True (T) or False (F).（判斷下列句子內容是否符合你所聽到的短文內容，符合的用"T" 表示，不符合的用"F" 表示。）（6分）

( ) 19. We're going to have a rest.

( ) 20. It will rain at night.

( ) 21. The temperature will fall below zero tomorrow morning.

( ) 22. Mr Wang is in hospital.

( ) 23. Students can watch TV until very late today.

( ) 24. The students are going to clean their classroom soon.

Ⅴ、Listen and fill in the blanks.（根據你所聽到的內容，用適當的單詞完成下面的句子。每空格限填一詞。）（6分）

● John is 12 years old and __25__ centimeters tall.

● His favourite food is fried chicken, __26__ and ice cream.

● He likes playing video games and __27__ TV for a long time.

● The doctor thinks that he is not very __28__ and he is 29.

● The doctor also thinks that John has a bad diet and needs to do more __30__ and eat more fruit and vegetables.

    25._____   26. _____   27. _____
    28._____   29. _____   30. _____

全新國中會考英語聽力精選(中)

Unit 4

I、Listen and choose the right picture.（根據你所聽到的內容，選出相應的圖片。）（6分）

A.

B.

C.

D.

E.

F.

G.

1. _____   2. _____   3. _____
4. _____   5. _____   6. _____

II、Listen to the dialogue and choose the best answer to the question you hear.（根據你所聽到的對話和問題，選出最恰當的答案。）（10分）

( ) 7. (A)For 11 hours. (B)For 9 hours.　(C)For 10 hours.　(D)For 8 hours.

( ) 8. (A)For 6 weeks.　(B)For 5 weeks.　(C)For 4 weeks.　(D)For 3 weeks.

( ) 9. (A)He's taking off his shoes.　(B)He's managing.
　　　 (C)He's catching the plane.　(D)He's packing.

( ) 10. (A)20 years old.　(B)22 years old.　(C)29 years old.　(D)30 years old.

( ) 11. (A)At home.　(B)At her friend's home.
　　　　(C)At his friend's home.　(D)At a shop.

( ) 12. (A)In a hotel.　(B)In a supermarket.
　　　　(C)In a restaurant.　(D)At a cinema.

( ) 13. (A)Tuesday.　(B)Sunday.　(C)Monday.　(D)Saturday.

( ) 14. (A)45 minutes.　(B)50 minutes.　(C)40 minutes.　(D)55 minutes.

( ) 15. (A)Yes, she can.　(B)Yes, she can't.
　　　　(C)No, she can.　(D)No, she can't.

( ) 16. (A)12.00 noon.　　(B)12.15 p.m.　　(C)11.45 a.m.　　(D)12.30 p.m.

Ⅲ、Listen to the passage and decide whether the following statements are True (T) or False (F). （判斷下列句子是否符合你所聽到的短文內容，符合的用 T 表示，不符合的用 F 表示。）（7分）

( ) 17. People in China do not use spoons.

( ) 18. Some people have trouble using chopsticks.

( ) 19. People in the UK do not usually eat chicken's feet or smelly tofu.

( ) 20. In Japan, people help themselves from plates of food in the middle of the table.

( ) 21. Most people in the UK use chopsticks.

( ) 22. In the UK, the cook cuts all the food into small pieces.

( ) 23. In the UK, people help themselves to the food.

Ⅳ、Listen to the dialogue and fill in the blanks. （根據你聽到的對話，完成下列內容，每空格限填一詞。）（7分）

What has Mary done?
- She has tried to get her mother to have some __24__ and 25
- She has asked her mother to have some __26__ soup
- She has asked her mother to drink some __27__ juice

What hasn't Mary's mother done?
- She hasn't eaten anything since __28__
- She hasn't __29__ well for __30__ nights

24. _____　25. _____　26. _____　27. _____

28. _____　29. _____　30. _____

全新國中會考英語聽力精選(中)

Unit 5

I、Listen and choose the right picture. (根據你所聽到的內容，選出相應的圖片。)（6分）

A.   B.   C.

D.   E.   F.   G.

1. _____   2. _____   3. _____
4. _____   5. _____   6. _____

II、Listen to the dialogue and choose the best answer to the question you hear. (根據你所聽到的對話和問題，選出最恰當的答案。)（10分）

(   ) 7. (A)On foot.   (B)By bus.   (C)By bike.   (D)By taxi.

(   ) 8. (A)At 2.00.   (B)At 2.05.   (C)At 2.10.   (D)At 2.20.

(   ) 9. (A)100 dollars. (B)50 dollars. (C)25 dollars. (D)20 dollars.

(   ) 10. (A)Some students.   (B)One student.
          (C)Some teachers.   (D)One teacher.

(   ) 11. (A)Terrible.   (B)Just so-so. (C)Well done.   (D)The best.

(   ) 12. (A)She doesn't like the film.   (B)She has seen the film.
          (C)She'd like to stay at home. (D)She likes watching TV.

(   ) 13. (A)In Shanghai Library.   (B)On Huaihai Road.
          (C)On the bus.   (D)On the underground.

(   ) 14. (A)In 1998.   (B)In 1999.   (C)In 2000.   (D)In 2001.

(   ) 15. (A)The man.   (B)The woman.
          (C)Both of them.   (D)Neither of them.

( ) 16. (A)Because he worked hard at English.
(B)Because he is not interested in English.
(C)Because he didn't pass the Chinese test.
(D)Because he failed in the English test.

III、Listen to the passage and decide whether the following statements are True (T) or False (F). (判斷下列句子是否符合你所聽到的短文內容，符合的用 T 表示，不符合的用 F 表示。) (7分)

( ) 17. Jean Champollion learned about twenty languages in his life.

( ) 18. Jean became very interested in ancient Egypt when he was young.

( ) 19. Jean started to study the Rosetta Stone in 1921.

( ) 20. Some scientists found the Rosetta Stone under the sand when Jean was a small boy.

( ) 21. There was a lot of strange writing on the stone.

( ) 22. Ancient Egyptian was a language with letters and words like English.

( ) 23. Jean thought that some of the signs on the Rosetta Stone told about sounds.

IV、Listen to the dialogue and fill in the blanks. (根據你聽到的對話，完成下列內容，每空格限填一詞。) (7分)

● There are more than __24__ different languages in the world.

● __25__ is the language with the most speakers （more than __26__ speakers）.

● __27__ is the second （more than __28__ speakers）.

● Some languages have a few speakers—about 40 or __29__.

● Some languages __30__ when grandparents pass away.

24. _____ 25. _____ 26. _____ 27. _____
28. _____ 29. _____ 30. _____

全新國中會考英語聽力精選(中)

Unit 6

Ⅰ、Listen and choose the right picture.（根據你所聽到的內容，選出相應的圖片。）（6分）

A.　　　　　　　B.　　　　　　　C.

D.　　　　　　E.　　　　　　　F.　　　　　　　G.

1. _____　　2. _____　　　　　　3. _____

4. _____　　5. _____　　　　　　6. _____

Ⅱ、Listen and choose the best response to the sentence you hear.（根據你所聽到的句子，選出最恰當的應答句。）（6分）

(　) 7. (A)On the table, please.　　　　(B)Opposite the sofa, please.
　　　　　(C)Take it away, please.　　　　(D)Bring it in, please.

(　) 8. (A)It's north of the map.　　　　(B)It's in the north on the map.
　　　　　(C)It's on the north of the map.　(D)It isn't here.

(　) 9. (A)Twice a week.　　　　　　(B)Two weeks.
　　　　　(C)About ten minutes.　　　　(D)10 o'clock.

(　) 10. (A)Yes, I do.　　　　　　　(B)No, I don't.
　　　　　(C)In the suburbs.　　　　　(D)I can't decide where to live.

(　) 11. (A)They usually run their dogs at the beach.
　　　　　(B)They watched the beautiful moon and stars at night.
　　　　　(C)They will visit the Great Wall in Beijing.
　　　　　(D)They have already finished their homework.

( ) 12. (A)It's February. (B)It's Friday.
(C)It's spring. (D)It's March 3.

Ⅲ、Listen to the dialogue and choose the best answer to the question you hear.（根據你所聽到的對話和問題，選出最恰當的答案。）（6分）

( ) 13. (A)Because he is not old.
(B)Because he eats less food.
(C)Because he works every day.
(D)Because he eats good food and works every day.

( ) 14. (A)An office. (B)Dr Black.
(C)A book on Chinese medicine. (D)A shelf.

( ) 15. (A)Three. (B)Four. (C)Five. (D)Six.

( ) 16. (A)She went to see her friends.
(B)She went to see her parents.
(C)She worked in a modern factory.
(D)She visited a beautiful farm.

( ) 17. (A)To go to a meeting.
(B)To take the underground.
(C)To see a film.
(D)To look for the underground station.

( ) 18. (A)To buy tickets. (B)To visit Fudan University.
(C)To sing English songs. (D)To attend an English evening.

Ⅳ、Listen to the passage and decide whether the following statements are True (T) or False (F).（判斷下列句子內容是否符合你所聽到的短文內容，符合的用"T"表示，不符合的用"F"表示。）（6分）

( ) 19. Jack is having a great time in San Diego.
( ) 20. Connie is going to Disneyland and Hollywood.
( ) 21. Connie will post Jack a card in Los Angeles.
( ) 22. Connie will go home by air on May 15.
( ) 23. The plane will arrive in Shanghai first.
( ) 24. Connie will visit her aunt in Hong Kong.

Ⅴ、Listen to the dialogue and complete the table.（根據你所聽到的對話內容，用適當的單詞或數字完成下面的表格。每空格限填一詞或數字。）（6分）

	Mrs Wang's old flat	The new flat she will buy

place	In the city centre __25__ but noisy	In the suburbs __26__
bedroom	2	__27__
kitchen	small	__28__
balcony	0	1
size	/	__29__ m^2
cost	/	__30__ yuan

25._____   26._____   27._____

28._____   29._____   30._____

全新國中會考英語聽力精選(中)

Unit 7

Ⅰ、Listen and choose the right picture.（根據你所聽到的內容,選出相應的圖片。）（6分）

A   B   C

D   E   F   G

1. _____   2. _____   3. _____

4. _____   5. _____   6. _____

Ⅱ、Listen to the dialogue and choose the best answer to the question. （根據你所聽到的對話和問題，選出最恰當的答案。)（10分）

( ) 7. (A)Milk.   (B)Eggs.   (C)Bacon.   (D)Bread.

( ) 8. (A)Nov. 2nd.   (B)Oct. 31st.   (C)Nov. 3rd.   (D)Nov. 4th.

( ) 9. (A)His workmate.   (B)His classmate.
        (C)His deskmate.   (D)His roommate.

( ) 10. (A)At the cinema.   (B)In the hospital.
         (C)At a library.   (D)At school.

( ) 11. (A)At 4 o'clock.   (B)At 3:30.   (C)At 3 o'clock.   (D)At 2:30.

( ) 12. (A)Exciting.   (B)Meaningful.   (C)Terrible.   (D)Interesting.

( ) 13. (A)A doctor.   (B)A policeman.   (C)A teacher.   (D)A worker.

( ) 14. (A)He smoked a lot.   (B)He began to smoke.
         (C)He had a sore throat.   (D)He threw the cigarettes away.

( ) 15. (A)In a restaurant.   (B)At school.
         (C)In the kitchen.   (D)In a flower market.

( ) 16. She is too old and she wants to give up learning more.

(B)She thinks it is wise to learn at one's early age.

(C)She won't stop learning till her death.

(D)She is afraid of learning too much as it wastes time.

III、Listen to the passage and tell whether the following statements are true or false. （判斷下列句子是否符合你聽到的短文內容,符合用 T 表示,不符合用 F 表示）（7分）

( ) 17. Jim lived alone in another town as he worked there.

( ) 18. Jim didn't like housework and he always made his flat dusty and untidy.

( ) 19. Mrs. Roper was introduced to Jim and came to see Jim the next morning.

( ) 20. Jim left a message on a paper to tell Mrs. Roper to clean the mirror.

( ) 21. Jim was always coughing badly whenever he breathed.

( ) 22. The cough medicine Mrs. Roper prepared would make Jim deeply moved.

( ) 23. Mrs. Roper misunderstood Jim's message.

IV、Listen to the passage and fill in the blanks with proper words. （聽短文,用最恰當的填空,每格限填一詞）（共7分）

● Healthy skin is __24__ to all kinds of people.

● Keeping your hands clean can stop germs from being __25__ to other places.

● We'd better use warm water and mild __26__ to wash hands.

● Remember to clean the __27__ under your arms or behind your ears during a bath.

● It is wise to wash your face once or twice __28__ with warm water.

● Drinking enough water makes your skin brighter and __29__.

● You will have fewer __30__ problems if you take good care of your skin.

24. _____   25. _____   26. _____   27. _____

28. _____   29. _____   30. _____

全新國中會考英語聽力精選(中)

Unit 8

> I、Listen and choose the right picture. (根據你所聽到的內容,選出相應的圖片。) (6分)

1. _____   2. _____   3. _____

4. _____   5. _____   6. _____

> II、Listen and choose the best response to the sentence you hear. (根據你所聽到的句子,選出最恰當的應答句。) (6分)

( ) 7.　(A)Yes, I do.　　　　　　　　(B)All right.
　　　　(C)I'd like a cup of coffee.　　(D)No, you needn't.

( ) 8.　(A)By foot.　　　　　　　　　(B)On foot.
　　　　(C)By my father's car.　　　　(D)On car.

( ) 9.　(A)You too.　　　　　　　　　(B)Thank you.
　　　　(C)Nice to meet you, too.　　　(D)Hello.

( ) 10.　(A)Thanks.　　　　　　　　　(B)No, it isn't.
　　　　 (C)Yes, I do.　　　　　　　　(D)No problem.

( ) 11.　(A)Each.　　　　　　　　　　(B)No, they aren't.
　　　　 (C)It's hard to say.　　　　　　(D)Yes, they are.

( ) 12.　(A)He will be good.　　　　　　(B)It's OK.
　　　　 (C)I'm sorry to hear that.　　　(D)That's great!

Ⅲ、Listen to the dialogue and choose the best answer to the question you hear.（根據你所聽到的對話和問題,選出最恰當的答案。）（6分）

( ) 13. (A)Hangzhou.   (B)Shanghai.
    (C)Beijing.   (D)Guangzhou.

( ) 14. (A)In a bank.   (B)At a restaurant.
    (C)In an office.   (D)At the airport.

( ) 15. (A)They are not delicious.   (B)He is hungry.
    (C)He is full.   (D)He doesn't like mooncakes.

( ) 16. (A)Two days later.   (B)Tomorrow.
    (C)Wednesday.   (D)Monday.

( ) 17. (A)Do some revision.   (B)Have a good rest.
    (C)Go to bed late.   (D)Do well in English.

( ) 18. (A)No, she isn't.   (B)No, she is.
    (C)Yes, she is.   (D)Yes, she isn't.

Ⅳ、Listen to the dialogue and decide whether the following statements are True (T) or False (F).（判斷下列句子內容是否符合你所聽到的對話內容,符合的用"T"表示,不符合的用"F"表示。）（6分）

( ) 19. New Zealand is in South America.

( ) 20. The old story in New Zealand says the God's parents created the world we live in.

( ) 21. The theme of the New Zealand Pavilion is "Better city, better life".

( ) 22. The pavilion has an area of 2,000 square meters.

( ) 23. There are four parts in the New Zealand Pavilion.

( ) 24. When people entered the pavilion, they could experience a day _____ in a New Zealand city.

Ⅴ、Listen and fill in the blanks.（根據你所聽到的內容,用適當的單詞完成下面的句子。每空格限填一詞。）（6分）

25. Usually, I couldn't give an _____ when people ask me the question: when is the best time to visit Shanghai?

26. _____ may be the best time to visit Shanghai.

27. There are many _____ during the Shanghai Travel _____.

28. There are also many other _____ events during the three weeks in Shanghai.

29. I believe that _____ of the beauty of Shanghai is its lights.

全新國中會考英語聽力精選(中)

Unit 9

I、Listen and choose the right picture.（根據你所聽到的內容，選出相應的圖片。）（6分）

A.

B.

C.

D.

E.

F.

G.

1. _____   2. _____   3. _____
4. _____   5. _____   6. _____

II、Listen and choose the best response to the sentence you hear.（根據你所聽到的句子，選出最恰當的應答句。）（6分）

(　) 7.　(A)What is an international food festival?
　　　　(B)Let's go to school to attend the food festival.
　　　　(C)Yes. It'll be great fun.
　　　　(D)Thank you very much.

(　) 8.　(A)I will sell fish and chips and raisin scones.
　　　　(B)I will sell pineapple fried rice and prawn cakes.
　　　　(C)I will sell hot dogs and apple pies.
　　　　(D)I will sell rice dumplings and moon cakes.

(　) 9.　(A)Thank you.　　　　　　(B)Of course.
　　　　(C)My pleasure.　　　　　(D)That's all right.

(　) 10.　(A)Yes, please.　　　　　(B)Yes, thank you.
　　　　(C)Yes, very good.　　　　(D)Yes, of course.

( ) 11. (A)Fifty yuan altogether. (B)There are ten.
(C)It's ten yuan. (D)Five kilograms.

( ) 12. (A)How are you? (B)We are in the USA now.
(C)Fine. And you? (D)Are you sure?

Ⅲ、Listen to the dialogue and choose the best answer to the question you hear.（根據你所聽到的對話和問題，選出最恰當的答案。）（6分）

( ) 13. (A)A glass of milk. (B)A glass of water.
(C)A cup of tea. (D)Nothing.

( ) 14. (A)She went to the cinema.
(B)He watched TV at home.
(C)He watched a football match.
(D)He saw a film and watched a football match.

( ) 15. (A)By bike. (B)On foot.
(C)By bus. (D)By underground.

( ) 16. (A)At the post office. (B)In the hospital.
(C)At the supermarket. (D)In the classroom.

( ) 17. (A)In the city. (B)In the village.
(C)In a small town. (D)In a quiet flat.

( ) 18. (A)Cookery lessons. (B)Computer lessons.
(C)Neither. (D)Both.

Ⅳ、Listen to the passage and decide whether the following statements are True (T) or False (F).（判斷下列句子內容是否符合你所聽到的短文內容，符合的用"T"表示，不符合的用"F"表示。）（6分）

( ) 19. Tom's parents have little money.

( ) 20. Tom's father can't buy a real football for him.

( ) 21. Both Tom and his father like playing football.

( ) 22. Tom is the best football player in the world.

( ) 23. Tom makes his living with his hands.

( ) 24. Tom's mother also likes playing football, too.

Ⅴ、Listen and fill in the blanks.（根據你所聽到的內容，用適當的單詞完成下面的句子。每空格限填一詞。）（6分）

● In __25__, there will be different kinds of materials for clothes.

● Clothes with special chemicals will never get __26__.

● People will save __27__ and money.

- Students won't need to __28__ about what to wear to school every day.

- Students will stay at home in front of their __29__.

- What do you think of the future life? Do you think it will be __30__?

25._____   26._____   27._____

28._____   29._____   30._____

全新國中會考英語聽力精選(中)

Unit 10

I、Listen and choose the right picture.（根據你所聽到的內容,選出相應的圖片。）（6分）

A   B   C

D   E   F   G

1. _____   2. _____   3. _____

4. _____   5. _____   6. _____

II、Listen and choose the best response to the sentence you hear.（根據你所聽到的句子,選出最恰當的應答句。）（6分）

( ) 7. (A)Shirts. (B)Sports shoes.
(C)Size medium. (D)Clothes.

( ) 8. (A)No, you can't. (B)The jeans are over there.
(C)Sure. (D)I don't like the color.

( ) 9. (A)It doesn't matter. (B)No, you don't.
(C)Yes, you do. (D)Don't bother me.

( ) 10. (A)What's the matter? (B)Sure. What time?
(C)Yes, I do. (D)The ball will be at my place.

( ) 11. (A)So do I. (B)So I do.
(C)Neither do I. (D)Neither I do.

( ) 12. (A)Three hours. (B)In three hours.
(C)At three o'clock. (D)Since three hours.

Ⅲ、Listen to the dialogue and choose the best answer to the question you hear. （根據你所聽到的對話和問題,選出最恰當的答案。）（6分）

( ) 13. (A)He doesn't like the style.   (B)He doesn't like the colour.
(C)The size is too big.   (D)The size is too small.

( ) 14. (A)4 yuan.   (B)8 yuan.
(C)12 yuan.   (D)14 yuan.

( ) 15. (A)A hat.   (B)Bracelet.
(C)Earrings.   (D)Glasses.

( ) 16. (A)For three years.   (B)For four years.
(C)For five years.   (D)For six years.

( ) 17. (A)10 dollars.   (B)15 dollars.
(C)20 dollars.   (D)25 dollars.

( ) 18. (A)At a clothes shop.   (B)In a restaurant.
(C)At an office.   (D)In the fire station.

Ⅳ、Listen to the dialogue and decide whether the following statements are True (T) or False (F). （判斷下列句子內容是否符合你所聽到的對話內容,符合的用"T"表示,不符合的用"F"表示。）（6分）

( ) 19. Lin Miaoke became famous after the 2008 Beijing Olympic Games.

( ) 20. Lin Miaoke sang the song "A Hymn to My motherland" at the opening ceremony.

( ) 21. She likes playing the piano and flute, but she can't dance.

( ) 22. She was six years old when she appeared in the TV advertisement with Liu Xiang.

( ) 23. The director Zhang Yimou chose her among all the children in Shanghai.

( ) 24. Now we can see her photos on many newspapers and magazines.

Ⅴ、Listen and fill in the blanks. （根據你所聽到的內容,用適當的單詞完成下面的句子。每空格限填一詞。）（6分）

25. The woman wants to buy a pair of _____ shoes.

26. The _____ pair is 200 dollars.

27. The white pair _____ the woman well.

28. The white pair is _____ dollars.

29. The woman likes the T-shirt with red _____.

30. The woman will pay _____ dollars for them.

Unit 11

Ⅰ、Listen and choose the right picture.（根據你所聽到的內容，選出相應的圖片。）（6分）

A.　　　　　　　　B.　　　　　　　　C.

D.　　　　E.　　　　F.　　　　G.

Ⅱ、Listen and choose the best response to the sentence you hear.（根據你所聽到的句子，選出最恰當的應答句。）（6分）

(　) 7. (A)Yes, I'd like to. 　　　　　(B)You're welcome.
　　　　(C)Yes, I will go with you. 　(D)I want to join you.

(　) 8. (A)I was in the Century Park. 　(B)I did some shopping on Friday.
　　　　(C)I visited People's Square. 　(D)My father drove me there.

(　) 9. (A)That's wonderful. 　(B)That's all.
　　　　(C)All right. 　　　　(D)That's OK.

(　) 10. (A)I'll be glad to. 　(B)Yes, I agree.
　　　　 (C)I'd like to. 　　 (D)Yes, I'd love to.

(　) 11. (A)So do mine. 　　(B)Neither do mine.
　　　　 (C)So are mine. 　 (D)Neither are mine.

(　) 12. (A)It's yours. 　　　(B)Here you are.
　　　　 (C)Here we are. 　 (D)Help yourself.

Ⅲ、Listen to the dialogue and choose the best answer to the question you hear.（根據你所聽到的對話和問題，選出最恰當的答案。）（6分）

( ) 13. (A)Water. (B)People. (C)Animals. (D)Land.

( ) 14. (A)My pet. (B)My grandma.
(C)My grandpa. (D)My parents.

( ) 15. (A)At home. (B)At school.
(C)In Pudong. (D)In the countryside.

( ) 16. (A)He never smiles. (B)She often helps us.
(C)He is kind to us. (D)She is a kind lady.

( ) 17. (A)Dick. (B)May. (C)Terry. (D)Lucy.

( ) 18. (A)Music. (B)Animal World.
(C)Sports news. (D)English news.

IV、Listen to the passage and decide whether the following statements are True (T) or False (F).（判斷下列句子內容是否符合你所聽到的短文內容，符合的用"T" 表示，不符合的用"F" 表示。）（6分）

( ) 19. The national holidays in different countries are on the same day.

( ) 20. Mexico's Independence Day is on July 14.

( ) 21. In the United States, people have parades on July 4.

( ) 22. In France, you don't need to pay money if you go to the concerts on their national holiday.

( ) 23. In France, people play mariachi music on Independence Day.

( ) 24. In the United States, France and Mexico, there are parades for Independence Day.

V、Listen to the dialogue and complete the table.（根據你所聽到的對話內容，用適當的單詞或數字完成下面的表格。每空格限填一詞或數字，或在方框內打勾。）（6分）Shopping

Things to buy	a pair of __25__ shoes	a T-shirt
Size	Size 8	Size 26
The colour she likes	__27__ Black□ White □	Red ☑ Blue □
Price	The black one $__28__ The white one __29__	The red one $80 The blue one $40
How much to pay altogether	$__30__	

25._____ 26. _____ 27. _____

28._____ 29. _____ 30. _____

Unit 12

Ⅰ、Listen and choose the right picture.（根據你所聽到的內容，選出相應的圖片。）（6分）

A.　　　　　　　　B.　　　　　　　　C.

D.　　　　　　　E.　　　　　　　F.　　　　　　　G.

1. _____　　　　2. _____　　　　3. _____

4. _____　　　　5. _____　　　　6. _____

Ⅱ、Listen to the dialogue and choose the best answer to the question you hear.（根據你所聽到的對話和問題，選出最恰當的答案。）（10分）

（　）7.　(A)He can carry the box.　(B)The box is very heavy.
　　　　　(C)Tom needs some help.　(D)He can't carry the box.

（　）8.　(A)She studied English and then watched TV.
　　　　　(B)She studied English instead of watching TV.
　　　　　(C)She watched TV after she studied English.
　　　　　(D)She studied English by watching TV.

（　）9.　(A)2.30.　　(B)2.40.　　(C)2.45.　　(D)3.00.

（　）10.　(A)The man.　　　　　　(B)The woman.
　　　　　(C)Both of them.　　　　(D)Neither of them.

（　）11.　(A)To have a talk.　　　　(B)To have an English lesson.
　　　　　(C)To attend a lecture.　　(D)To play football.

（　）12.　(A)To buy a dictionary.
　　　　　(B)To look up the word in the dictionary.

(C)To borrow a dictionary.

(D)To ask the teacher for help.

( ) 13. (A)To her office.   (B)To school.

(C)To the market.   (D)To stay for supper.

( ) 14. (A)40,000.   (B)30,000.   (C)20,000.   (D)10,000.

( ) 15. (A)Some chicken.   (B)Some chocolate.

(C)Some fruit.   (D)Some vegetables.

( ) 16. (A)The doctor.   (B)The headmaster.

(C)The teacher.   (D)The student.

Ⅲ、Listen to the passage and decide whether the following statements are True (T) or False (F).（判斷下列句子是否符合你所聽到的短文內容，符合的用 T 表示，不符合的用 F 表示。）（7分）

( ) 17. San Francisco is a cold, dark place.

( ) 18. According to the passage, it is a long way to walk to the top of the hill if you want to look down on San Francisco Bay.

( ) 19. Only sports-lovers or food-lovers should visit San Francisco.

( ) 20. Golden Gate Park is near Golden Gate Bridge.

( ) 21. You can find a Japanese Tea Garden in the Golden Gate Park.

( ) 22. In Chinatown you can only get hot Sichuan food.

( ) 23. San Francisco's Chinatown is bigger than London's.

Ⅳ、Listen to the passage and fill in the blanks.（根據你聽到的短文，完成下列內容，每空格限填一詞。）（7分）

About Bangkok — the capital of Thailand

● Streets in Bangkok are __24__

People must leave __25__ if they go to work in the morning

● Tuk-tuks are like little __26__ with __27__ wheels

● Bangkok is famous for its Floating __28__

People sell fruit and vegetables from their __29__

● Thai food are usually very __30__

24. _____   25. _____   26. _____   27. _____

28. _____   29. _____   30. _____

全新國中會考英語聽力精選(中)

Unit 13

I、Listen and choose the right picture.（根據你所聽到的內容,選出相應的圖片。）（6分）

A   B   C

D   E   F   G

1. _____   2. _____   3. _____
4. _____   5. _____   6. _____

II、Listen and choose the best response to the sentence you hear.（根據你所聽到的句子,選出最恰當的應答句。）（6分）

( ) 7.   (A)So do mine.   (B)Neither do mine.
         (C)So is mine.   (D)Neither is mine.

( ) 8.   (A)Yes, I can.   (B)No, I can't.
         (C)I'm sorry to have bothered you.   (D)Yes, I could.

( ) 9.   (A)Yes, I am.   (B)Yes, he is.
         (C)Yes, speaking.   (D)I'm Mr Brown.

( ) 10. (A)What a pity!   (B)What fun!
         (C)I know.   (D)I don't think so.

( ) 11. (A)Certainly.   (B)That's all right.
         (C)That's right.   (D)You're welcome.

( ) 12. (A)In a day.   (B)Twice a day.
         (C)At 7 o'clock.   (D)For two times.

Ⅲ、Listen to the dialogue and choose the best answer to the question you hear.（根據你所聽到的對話和問題,選出最恰當的答案。）（6分）

( ) 13.   (A)At the weekend.   (B)On weekdays.
             (C)On Saturday.   (D)On Sunday.

( ) 14.   (A)6624594.   (B)6627594.
             (C)6627495.   (D)6624495.

( ) 15.   (A)They are looking at the photo.   (B)They are visiting a
                                          kindergarten.
             (C)They are talking to an aunt.   (D)They are watching TV.

( ) 16.   (A)A student.   (B)A nurse.
             (C)A teacher.   (D)A doctor.

( ) 17.   (A)10:45.   (B)9:45.
             (C)11:45.   (D)8:45.

( ) 18.   (A)To a post office.   (B)To a food shop.
             (C)To a library.   (D)To a bank.

Ⅳ、Listen to the dialogue and decide whether the following statements are True (T) or False (F).（判斷下列句子內容是否符合你所聽到的對話內容,符合的用"T"表示,不符合的用"F"表示。）（6分）

( ) 19.   Forests are important to us.

( ) 20.   Trees only provide food for animals.

( ) 21.   Animals will die quickly without trees.

( ) 22.   Cans are made of clay.

( ) 23.   Glass is made from sand on the beaches.

( ) 24.   Everything we use in our daily life comes from trees and land.

Ⅴ、Listen and fill in the blanks.（根據你所聽到的內容,用適當的單詞完成下面的句子。每空格限填一詞。）（6分）

25. The mudslide happened in early _____ in Gansu.

26. Many people were _____.

27. About _____ people died.

28. We had a _____ class just now.

29. We've decided to _____ some money for them.

30. The boy's father is an _____.

全新國中會考英語聽力精選(中)

Unit 14

Ⅰ、Listen and choose the right picture.（根據你所聽到的內容，選出相應的圖片。）（6分）

A.   B.   C.

D.   E.   F.   G.

1. _____   2. _____   3. _____

4. _____   5. _____   6. _____

Ⅱ、Listen to the dialogue and choose the best answer to the question you hear.（根據你所聽到的對話和問題，選出最恰當的答案。）（10分）

(   ) 7.   (A)At 2.00.   (B)At 2.30.   (C)At 3.00.   (D)At 3.30.

(   ) 8.   (A)In a library.   (B)In a CD shop.
            (C)In a theatre.   (D)In a restaurant.

(   ) 9.   (A)By bus.   (B)By bike.   (C)On foot.   (D)By car.

(   ) 10.   (A)Because he has to look after his sister.
            (B)Because he will visit Mary.
            (C)Because he has visited Alice.
            (D)Because she will visit her.

(   ) 11.   (A)To have a picnic.   (B)To take some films.
            (C)To go on a trip.   (D)To buy some food.

(   ) 12.   (A)Mum and son.   (B)Teacher and student.
            (C)Waiter and customer.   (D)Host and guest.

(   ) 13.   (A)Dentist.   (B)Nurse.   (C)Teacher.   (D)Doctor.

(   ) 14.   (A)64580023.   (B)62580023.   (C)64850023.   (D)62850023.

( ) 15. (A)Coffee and bread. (B)Beef and pork.
(C)Meat. (D)Nothing.

( ) 16. (A)On the phone. (B)At Jenny's home.
(C)At the computer room. (D)At Tom's home.

Ⅲ、Listen to the passage and decide whether the following statements are True (T) or False (F).（判斷下列句子是否符合你所聽到的短文內容，符合的用 T 表示，不符合的用 F 表示。）（7分）

( ) 17. The speakers asked three questions at the beginning and the answers to these questions are all "No".

( ) 18. Grandmother often tells the speaker some stories about her childhood.

( ) 19. It seems that in the city people lived in a cleaner environment many years ago.

( ) 20. The speaker told us that people are doing something bad to the city now.

( ) 21. The speaker thought that the Earth is in trouble.

( ) 22. The speaker seemed to be a member of an organization which helps protect the environment.

( ) 23. The speaker suggested we reuse plastic bags for shopping.

Ⅳ、Listen to the dialogue and fill in the blanks.（根據你聽到的對話，完成下列內容，每空格限填一詞。）（7分）

QUESTIONNAIRE: How do you feel about these __24__?

Your choices:

Anot worried at all

Ba __25__ worried

Cvery worried

Question 1: People throwing __26__ in parks, streets and __27__ places.

Your answer: ☐

Question 2: People making a lot of __28__.

Your answer: ☐

Question 3: People __29__ the water and the air.

Your answer: ☐

Question 4: A lot of __30__ on the road.

Your answer: ☐

24. _____ 25. _____ 26. _____ 27. _____

28. _____ 29. _____ 30. _____

Unit 15

I、Listen and choose the right picture. (根據你所聽到的內容，選出相應的圖片) (5分)

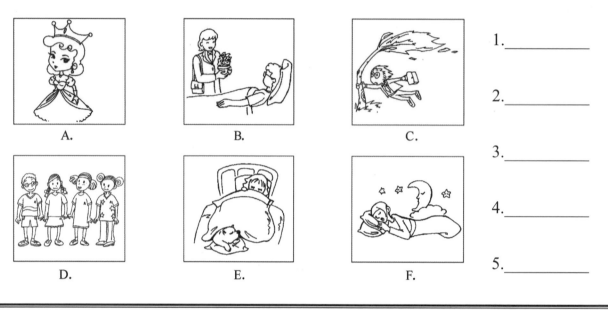

A.　　　　　B.　　　　　C.

D.　　　　　E.　　　　　F.

1.＿＿＿＿＿＿

2.＿＿＿＿＿＿

3.＿＿＿＿＿＿

4.＿＿＿＿＿＿

5.＿＿＿＿＿＿

II、Listen and choose the right word you hear in each sentence. (根據你所聽到的句子，選出正確的單字。) (5分)

( ) 7.　(A)smell　　(B)smile　　(C)small　　(D)smart

( ) 8.　(A)night　　(B)nice　　(C)note　　(D)nose

( ) 9.　(A)from　　(B)front　　(C)frog　　(D)fog

( ) 10.　(A)road　　(B)read　　(C)rope　　(D)route

( ) 11.　(A)bake　　(B)back　　(C)baker　　(D)bad

III、Listen and choose the best response to the sentence you hear. (根據你所聽到的句子，選出最恰當的應答句。) (5分)

( ) 12.　(A)We have no class.　　　　(B)I'm in Class One.
　　　　　(C)At eight in the morning.　(D)In the evening.

( ) 13.　(A)My watch is slow.　　　(B)Yours is ten minutes fast.
　　　　　(C)Maybe I know.　　　　(D)It's five twenty-five.

( ) 14.　(A)I don't know the bus stop.　(B)The bus doesn't stop here.
　　　　　(C)Only cars stop here.　　　(D)At the next corner.

( ) 15.　(A)It's Sunday.　　　　　(B)It's September the third.

(C)It's a hot day.   (D)It's our holiday.

(   ) 16. (A)You're welcome.   (B)All right.

             (C)Yes, please.   (D)No, I needn't.

IV、Listen to the dialogue and choose the best answer to the question you hear. （根據你所聽到的對話和問題，選出最恰當的答案。）（5分）

(   ) 17. (A)August.   (B)July.

             (C)June.   (D)June and August.

(   ) 18. (A)Tom.   (B)Tim.

             (C)Nancy.   (D)The boy.

(   ) 19. (A)In Shanghai.   (B)In Nanjing.

             (C)In Beijing.   (D)In Tianjin.

(   ) 20. (A)In a shop.   (B)In the library.

             (C)On the playground.   (D)In the hospital.

(   ) 21. (A)Room 405.   (B)Room 404.

             (C)Room 504.   (D)Room 505.

V、Listen to the passage and decide whether the following statements are True (T) or False (F). （判斷下列句子內容是否符合你所聽到的短文內容，符合的用 T 表示，不符合的用 F 表示。）（5分）

(   ) 22. Alice loves dressing up and she will be very beautiful.

(   ) 23. She will possibly be a model or a singer.

(   ) 24. Her mother also wants her to be a model or a singer.

(   ) 25. She will be 170 centimetres tall and 54 kilograms heavy.

(   ) 26. Alice studies hard and she is good at English.

VI、Listen to the dialogue and complete the notes. （根據你所聽到的對話內容，用適當的單詞完成下面的筆記。每空格限填一個單詞。）（5分）

- Jack will be __26__ centimetres taller.
- Jack will weigh __27__ kilograms.
- Jack will be __28__.
- Jack will be good at __29__.
- Jack will probably be a__30__.

26._____   27. _____   28. _____

29._____   30. _____

全新國中會考英語聽力精選(中)原文及參考答案

Unit 1

I、Listen and choose the right picture. (根據你所聽到的內容，選出相應的圖片。) (6分)

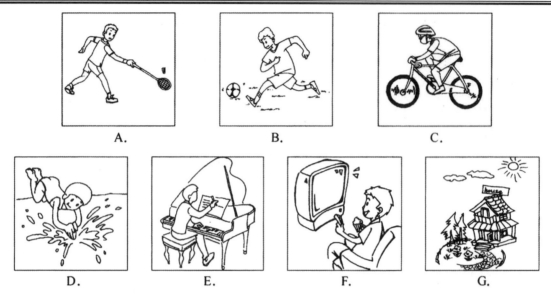

A.　　B.　　C.

D.　　E.　　F.　　G.

1. Alice lived in a villa in the countryside with her large family.
   (Alice 和她的大家庭住在鄉村的別墅。)
   答案：(G)

2. Simon often practises cycling in the stadium after class.
   (Simon 課後常常在體育場練習騎腳踏車。)
   答案：(C)

3. Would you like to play badminton with me tomorrow? (你明天可以跟我去打羽毛球嗎？)
   答案：(A)

4. I have a piano lesson from eight to nine this evening. I can't go to the cinema with you.
   (今天晚上八點到九點我有鋼琴課。我不能跟你去看電影。)
   答案：(E)

5. Judy is a diver. She goes to the swimming pool for training every day.
   (Judy 是潛水員。她每天去游泳池接受訓練。)
   答案：(D)

6. How about watching TV now? I know there's a new play on tonight.
   現在看電視如何？我知道今天晚上有一齣新的戲劇。
   答案：(F)

7. W: There are three people in my family. What about yours, John?

    (W: 我家有三個人。John，你呢？)

    M: Five, Kate.(M: Kate，有五個人。)

    Question: Whose family is smaller? (問題：誰的家庭比較小？)

    (A)John's family is bigger.(John 的家庭比較大。)

    (B)John's family is smaller. (John 的家庭比較小。)

    (C)Kate's family is bigger(Kate 的家庭比較大。)

    (D)Kate's family is smaller. (Kate 的家庭比較小。)

    答案：(D)

8. M: These mooncakes are very delicious. Please have a taste, Jane.

    (M: 這些月餅非常好吃。請嚐嚐看，Jane。)

    W: No, thanks. I can't eat any more.(W: 不了，謝謝。我吃不下了。)

    Question: Is Jane hungry? (問題：Jane 餓嗎？)

    (A)Yes, I am.(是的，我餓了。)   (B)Yes, she is. (是的，她餓了。)

    (C)No, I'm not. (不，我不。)   (D)No, she isn't. (不，她不餓。)

    答案：(D)

9. W: Are you good at swimming, Tom?(W: Tom, 你擅長游泳嗎？)

    M: Yes, but I like tennis best.(M: 是，但是我最喜歡網球。)

    Question: What is Tom's favourite sport? (問題：Tom 最喜歡的運動是甚麼？)

    (A)Football.(足球)   (B)Swimming.(游泳)

    (C)Tennis.(網球)   (D)Table tennis.(桌球)

    答案：(C)

10. W: May I help you, sir? Do you need any fruit?

    (M: 先生，我能為你服務嗎？你需要水果嗎？)

    M: Let me see. Ah, yes! I want two kilograms of bananas.

    (M: 讓我想想。啊，對了！我要兩公斤的香蕉。)

    Question: Where are they now? (問題：他們現在哪裡？)

    (A)They are in a clothes shop.(他們在服裝店。)

    (B)They are at the fruit stall.(他們在水果攤。)

    (C)They are in the cinema.(他們在電影院。)

    (D)They are at the hospital.(他們在醫院。)

    答案：(B)

11. W: Were you in Guangzhou last week?(W: 你上星期在廣州嗎？)

    M: Yes, I was. I went there for a meeting.(M: 是的，我在。我去那兒參加一場會議。)

    Question: Why did the man go to Guangzhou last week?

    (問題：那男人上星期為什麼去廣州？)

(A)He was travelling there.(他去那兒旅行。)

(B)He had a meeting there.(他在那兒有場會議。)

(C)He went to meet the woman there.(他去那兒和一個女人見面。)

(D)He visited some relatives there.(他去那兒拜訪一些親戚。)

答案：(B)

12. W: I have got two tickets for the football match, Danny. Let's go together, shall we?

    (W: Danny，我有兩張足球票。我們一起去看，好嗎？)

    M: Thank you, I'd love to. When?(M: 謝謝，我很樂意。甚麼時候呢？)

    W: On Sunday evening.(W: 星期天晚上。)

    M: Oh! I am afraid I won't be free at that time.(M: 喔！我那時候恐怕沒空。)

    W: What a pity!(W: 真可惜！)

    Question: Will Danny watch the football match? (問題：Danny 會去看足球賽嗎？)

    (A)Yes, he will.(是的，他會去。)　　　(B)No, he won't.(不，他不去。)

    (C)Yes, he did.(是的，他去了。)　　　(D)No, he didn't.(不，他沒去。)

    答案：(B)

13. W: I left my raincoat in the classroom. I will go back to get it. Wait, Tom!

    (W: 我把雨衣留在教室了。我要去把它拿回來。Tom，等等我！)

    M: No, you needn't. The weather report says it will clear up soon.

    (M: 你不需要去。氣象報告說馬上就放晴了。)

    Question: What did Tom advise the girl to do? (問題：Tom 建議那女孩做甚麼？)

    (A)He advised her to take her raincoat with her.(他建議她去拿雨衣。)

    (B)He advised her to take her umbrella with her.(他建議她去拿雨傘。)

    (C)He advised her not to take her umbrella with her.(他建議她不要去拿雨傘。)

    (D)He advised her not to take her raincoat with her.(他建議她不要去拿雨衣。)

    答案：(D)

14. M: Which is the most serious kind of pollution, noise pollution, water pollution, land pollution or air pollution?(M: 哪一種汙染最嚴重，噪音汙染、水汙染、土壤汙染、還是空氣汙染？)

    W: I think air pollution is the most serious kind of pollution.

    (W: 我認為空氣汙染是最嚴重的污染。)

    Question: What is the most serious kind of pollution according to the woman?

    (問題：根據那女人，哪一種是最嚴重的污染。)

    (A)Noise pollution.(噪音汙染。)　　　(B)Air pollution.(空氣汙染。)

    (C)Water pollution.(水汙染。)　　　(D)Land pollution.(土壤汙染。)

    答案：(B)

15. W: Where were you between 7 and 10 o'clock last night?

    (W: 昨天晚上七點到十點之間你在哪裡？)

    M: I went to the cinema with my friend, Andrew.(M:我跟朋友 Andrew 去看電影。)

W: Where did you meet him?(W: 你在哪裡跟他碰面？)

M: He came to my flat.(M: 他來我公寓。)

W: When?(W: 甚麼時候？)

M: At around half past six in the evening.(M: 差不多晚上六點半。)

Question: Where was Andrew at about half past six yesterday evening?

(問題：昨天晚上六點半左右，Andrew 在哪裡？)

(A)At the boy's flat.(在那男孩的公寓。) (B)At the girl's flat.(在那女孩的公寓。)

(C)At the cinema.(在電影院。) (D)At his own home.(在他家。)

答案：(A)

16. M: Tomorrow is Saturday. We needn't work in the office. I want to see a film. Will you go with me?(M: 明天是星期六。我們不需要在辦公室上班。我想去看電影。你要跟我去嗎？)

W: My brother has asked me to play tennis, but I want to breathe some fresh air.

(W: 我哥哥找我去打網球，但是我想去呼吸新鮮空氣。)

Question: What is the possible relationship between the two speakers?

(問題：這兩個談話者之間可能是甚麼樣的關係？)

(A)Brother and sister.(兄弟姊妹。) (B)Father and daughter.(父女。)

(C)Son and mother.(母子。) (D)Workmates.(同事。)

答案：(D)

Ⅲ、Listen to the letter and decide whether the following statements are True (T) or False (F).（判斷下列句子是否符合你所聽到的信件的內容，符合的用 T 表示，不符合的用 F 表示。）（7分）

Dear Kelly,

Do you like this photo of me with my school friends? I am in glasses. Can you see me? On the right is Sally. She is British. She is my best friend at school. She is always happy to help everyone. On the left is Alice. I play table tennis with her every afternoon.

The boys stand behind us. Danny wears glasses too. He is a painter. His paintings are very beautiful. He is also a basketball player on the school team. Our school team often wins the Middle School Championship in the city. Peter is a very good swimmer. He practises every morning and night. He wants to be one of the best swimmers in the world. He is the boy next to Jack. Jack is the tallest boy in the class. He is good at tennis. His favourite tennis player is Roger Federer. Bill is the boy on the right. He is not very good at sports, but he is very friendly to everyone around him. We all like him a lot.

Please write to me soon and tell me about your friends.

Love,
Kitty

親愛的 Kelly，

　　妳喜歡這張我和學校朋友的合照嗎？我戴眼鏡。你看到我了嗎？右邊的是 Sally。她是英國人。她是我在學校最好的朋友。她總是很樂意幫助他人。左邊的是 Alice。我跟她每天下午一起打桌球。

　　男生們站在我們的後面。Danny 也戴眼鏡。他是一位畫家。他的畫作非常漂亮。他也是校隊的籃球選手。我們的校隊經常贏得本市的中學冠軍。Peter 是一位很棒的游泳選手。他每天早晚練習。他想成為世界上最棒的游泳選手之一。他是站在 Jack 隔壁的那個男生。Jack 是班上最高的男生。他擅長網球。他最喜歡的網球選手是 Roger Federer。Bill 是在右邊的那個男生。他不擅長運動，但是他對他身邊的每個人都很友善。我們都很喜歡他。

　　請快回信，跟我聊聊你的朋友。

愛你的，Kitty

17. Kitty receives a letter from Kelly. (Kitty 收到一封 Kelly 寫來的信。)
　　答案：(F 錯)

18. Sally, who stands on the right of Kitty, is from the UK.(站在 Kitty 右邊的 Sally 是英國人。)
　　答案： (T 對)

19. Kelly usually plays table tennis with Alice at school. (Kelly 常常在學校和 Alice 一起打桌球。)
　　答案：(F 錯)

20. Danny can draw very well. (Danny 畫圖畫得非常好。)
　　答案： (T 對)

21. Peter practises playing tennis every day.(Peter 每天練習打網球。)
　　答案：(F 錯)

22. Bill is quite good at sports. (Bill 相當擅長於運動。)
　　答案：(F 錯)

23. Kitty wants to know something about Kelly's friends.
　　(Kitty 想知道一些關於 Kelly 的朋友的事。)
　　答案：(T 對)

IV、Listen to the passage and fill in the blanks.（根據你聽到的短文，完成下列內容，每空格限填一詞。）（7 分）

　　Jane is my classmate. She is twelve years old and one hundred and sixty centimetres tall. She is an American girl. She is from New York. She has big blue eyes. Her hair is not black. It is brown. Jane speaks English and she can speak a little Chinese, too. Both of her parents are engineers. She has a sister. Her name is Helen. She is twenty-one years old. She is an architect in New York.

　　It is Tuesday. Jane and I are very busy. Jane is carrying a bucket of water to the classroom. The water is heavy. I am washing the blackboard and Jane is cleaning the floor.

Soon, the classroom is nice and clean.

Jane 是我同學。她十二歲,高一百六十公分。她是一個美國女孩。她從紐約來。她有大大的藍眼睛。她的頭髮不是黑色的,而是棕色的。Jane 說英文,她也會說一點中文。她的父母都是工程師。她有一個姊姊。她的名字是 Helen。她二十一歲。她是紐約的建築師。

今天星期二。Jane 和我非常忙。Jane 要搬一桶水去教室。水非常重。我在清洗黑板,Jane 在清掃地板。教室很快的就會很乾淨。

- Jane is __24__ years old. (Jane___歲。)
- Jane is __25__ centimetres tall. (Jane 高___公分。)
- Jane has __26__ hair. (Jane 有____的頭髮。)
- Jane speaks English and she can speak a little __27__. (Jane 說英文,她會說一點____。)
- Jane's parents work as __28__. (Jane 的父母擔任____。)
- Jane's sister, Helen is an __29__. (Jane 的姊姊 Helen 是一位____。)
- Jane is __30__ the floor in the classroom. (Jane 在____教室的地板。)

24. 答案:12/twelve (十二)
25. 答案:160/one hundred and sixty (一百六十)
26. 答案:brown (棕色)
27. 答案:Chinese (中文)
28. 答案:engineers (工程師)
29. 答案:architect (建築師)
30. 答案:cleaning (清理/清掃)

Unit 2

> Ⅰ、Listen and choose the right picture.（根據你所聽到的內容,選出相應的圖片。）（6分）

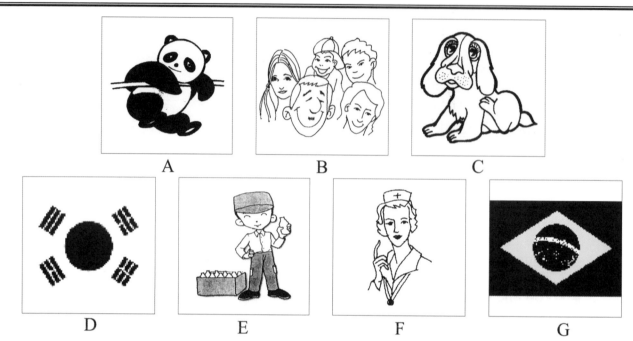

1. People should treat dogs as our friends because they are lovely and helpful.
   （人們應該把狗當作是我們的朋友，因為牠們很可愛也很有幫助。）
   答案：(C)

2. Is the Brazil football team the champion of the World Cup 2010?
   （巴西足球隊是 2010 世界杯的冠軍嗎？）
   答案：(G)

3. Look! The panda from Woolong is playing happily at Shanghai Wild Animal Park.
   （看！從臥龍來的熊貓在上海野生動物園快樂的玩耍。）
   答案：(A)

4. Mr Li is a milkman. He delivers milk to people in this neighborhood.
   （Li 先生是送奶工人。他為這附近的人送牛奶。）
   答案：(E)

5. Vets are doctors who take care of sick animals.（獸醫是照顧生病動物的醫生。）
   答案：(F)

6. John made friends with many teenagers and this is a picture of them.

（John 與許多青少年交朋友，這是他們的照片。）

答案：(B)

II、**Listen and choose the best response to the sentence you hear.**（根據你所聽到的句子,選出最恰當的應答句。）（6分）

7. Don't forget your homework.（別忘了你的功課。）
   (A)Yes, I will.（好，我會忘記。）   (B)No, I won't.（不，我不會忘記。）
   (C)Yes, I won't.（好，我不會忘記。）   (D)No, I will.（不，我會忘記。）
   答案：(B)

8. Where have you been during the summer holiday?（暑假期間你去了哪裡？）
   (A)At three in the morning.（早上三點。）
   (B)In Shanghai.（在上海。）
   (C)With my parents.（和我父母。）
   (D)Taiwan.（台灣。）
   答案：(D)

9. What is your nationality?（你的國籍是？）
   (A)Germany.（德國。）   (B)China.（中國。）
   (C)American.（美國人。）   (D)Australia.（澳洲。）
   答案：(C)

10. My brother has got a pen-friend from Canada.（我哥哥有一個來自加拿大的筆友。）
    (A)So do I.（我也有。）   (B)Neither do I.（我也沒有。）
    (C)So have I.（我也有。）   (D)Neither haven't I.（我也沒有。）
    答案：(C)

11. Mum, shall we invite these foreign friends home?
    （媽，我們邀請這些外國朋友來家裡好嗎？）
    (A)That's a good idea.（那是個好主意。）
    (B)I'm afraid you are wrong.（我恐怕你錯了。）
    (C)That's all right.（沒關係。）
    (D)You are welcome.（不客氣。）
    答案：(A)

12. Give me your passport please, sir.（先生，請給我你的護照。）
    (A)Here is it.（在這裡。）   (B)Here you are.（給你/在這裡。）
    (C)It is here.（它在這裡。）   (D)No, I don't.（不，我不給。）
    答案：(B)

13. W: It is said that you made a new friend on the Internet.

    （W: 聽說你在網路上交了一個新朋友。）

    M: Yes, Mandy is an English engineer and she works in a French car factory.

    （M: 是的，Mandy 是一位英國工程師，她在一家法國汽車工廠上班。）

    Q: What nationality is Mandy?（Q: Many 的國籍是？）

    (A)German.（德國人。）　　　　　　(B)American.（美國人。）

    (C)English.（英國人。）　　　　　　(D)French.（法國人。）

    答案：(C)

14. W: Excuse me, where's the teachers' office?（W: 不好意思，老師辦公室在哪裡？）

    M: It's on the third floor. There is a lab on its right. On its left there is a library.

    （M: 在三樓。它的右邊有一間實驗室。左邊有一間圖書館。）

    Q: What is the lady looking for?（Q: 那位小姐在找甚麼？）

    (A)The teachers' office.（老師辦公室。）

    (B)On the third floor.（在三樓。）

    (C)The library.（圖書館。）

    (D)The lab.（實驗室。）

    答案：(A)

15. W: Hi, Bob. I am going to hold a birthday party at home this Saturday. Are you free to come?（W: 嗨，Bob。這個星期天我要在家辦一場生日派對。你有空來嗎？）

    M: I'd love to, but you know my parents will come back from their trip to Australia on Saturday morning. I need to meet them at the airport.

    （M: 我想去，但是我爸媽去澳洲旅行，星期六早上就回來了。我要去機場接他們。）

    W: Oh, what a pity!（W: 喔，好可惜喔！）

    Q: When will the girl hold her birthday party?

    （Q: 那個女孩甚麼時候舉辦她的生日派對？）

    (A)This Saturday.（這個星期六。）

    (B)This Sunday morning.（這個星期天早上。）

    (C)At the airport.（在機場。）

    (D)At home.（在家。）

    答案：(A)

16. W: Peter, how many girl students are there in your class?

    （W: Peter，你班上有幾個女學生？）

    M: There are 45 students in all. One-third of them are girls.

（M: 一共有四十五個學生。三分之一是女生。）

Q: How many boy students are there in Peter's class?

（Q: Peter 的班上有多少男學生？）

(A)45.   (B)15.   (C)30.   (D)35.

答案：(C)

17. M: Welcome to Radisson. What can I do for you, Madam?

（M: 歡迎來 Radisson。這位女士，我能為妳效勞嗎？）

W: I have booked a room here on the phone.（W: 我電話預約了一間房間。）

M: Let me check the details. Your name please, Madam.

（M: 讓我核對一下內容。女士，請教你的大名。）

W: Sophie Brown.（W: Sophie Brown。）

Q: Where does this dialogue probably take place?

（Q: 這段對話大概在哪裡發生？）

(A)At a hotel.（在旅館。）   (B)At a clinic.（在診所。）

(C)In a supermarket.（在超級市場。）   (D)In a shopping mall.（在購物中心。）

答案：(A)

18. M: Where have you been during the holiday, Jane?

（M: Jane，假期期間妳去了哪裡？）

W: I have been to the US to visit my grandparents.

（W: 我去美國探望我的祖父母。）

M: Oh! It must be very interesting. What did you do there?

（M: 喔！那一定很有趣。妳在那裡做了些甚麼？）

W: I stayed in New York with my grandparents for two weeks. Then we went to the Disney Park in Los Angeles.

（W: 我與我的祖父母在紐約待了兩個星期。然後我們去洛杉磯的迪士尼樂園。）

M: What an amazing journey!（M: 好精采的旅程啊！）

Q: How many cities has Jane visited?（Q: Jane 造訪了幾個城市？）

(A)1.   (B)2.   (C)3.   (D)4.

答案：(B)

IV、Listen to the dialogue and decide whether the following statements are True (T) or False (F).（判斷下列句子內容是否符合你所聽到的對話內容,符合的用"T"表示,不符合的用"F"表示。）（6分）

I have a pen friend called Danny. He is a boy from Australia. Danny is 22 years old. His favourite interests are taking photos and collecting coins. He works as an architect in a company. Danny starts work at nine o'clock every morning and finishes his work at a quarter past five in the afternoon. But sometimes he needs to work for a long time at home. He writes letters to me twice a month. We share happiness with each other.

　　我有一個筆友叫 Danny。他是來自澳洲的男孩。Danny 二十二歲。他最大的興趣就是拍照和蒐集錢幣。他在一家公司擔任建築師的工作。Danny 每天早上九點開始上班，下午五點十五分結束工作。但是有時候他需要長時在家工作。他一個月寫兩封信給我。我們分享彼此的快樂。

19. Danny is an Australian.（Danny 是澳洲人。）

　　答案：(T 對)

20. One of his favorite interests is playing the guitar.
　　（他最喜歡的興趣之一是彈吉他。）

　　答案：(F 錯)

21. His job is to draw plans of buildings.（他的工作是畫建築物的平面圖。）

　　答案：(T 對)

22. Danny has to work over 8 hours every day. （Danny 每天工作超過八小時。）

　　答案：(T 對)

23. He never takes work home.（他從不把工作帶回家。）

　　答案：(F 錯)

24. We keep in touch with each other twice a month.（我們一個月與對方聯絡兩次。）

　　答案：(T 對)

V、Listen and fill in the blanks.（根據你所聽到的內容,用適當的單詞完成下面的句子。每空格限填一詞。）（6分）

W: Can I help you?（W: 我能為你效勞嗎？）

M: Yes, I'd like a ticket to Thailand.（M: 是的。我想要買一張去泰國的票。）

W: For today, the third of February?（W: 是今天二月三日的票嗎？）

M: No, tomorrow morning.（M: 不，明天早上。）

W: There's a flight and you'll get there at half past five tomorrow afternoon. Is that OK?（W: 明天下午五點半有一班到泰國的班機。可以嗎？）

M: Can I have it earlier? I will have a meeting at three in the afternoon.
　（M: 我想要早一點的可以嗎？我下午三點有個會議。）

W: I'm afraid not. If you want a night flight...
　（W: 恐怕不行。如果你想要夜航班機的話...）

M: A night flight?（M: 夜航班機？）

W: Yes, with United Airlines at a quarter to ten. You'll get there at a quarter past six tomorrow morning. Is that too early?

（W: 是的，九點四十五分的聯合航空。你將會在明天早上六點十五分抵達。會不會太早？）

M: Let me see. How much does it cost?（M: 讓我想想看。要多少錢呢？）

W: Seven hundred and eighty-six yuan. The flight number is 2316, at Gate 7, New York City Airport.

（W: 七百八十六元。班機號碼是 2316，在紐約市機場的七號登機門。）

M: Pretty good.（M: 挺不錯的。）

W: OK. Your name, please?（W: 好。請教你的大名。）

M: My name's Jack Li.（M: 我的名字是 Jack Li。）

W: Thank you, Mr. Li. Check-in time is two hours before you get on the plane. Have a good trip.

（W: 謝謝你，Li 先生。報到時間是登機前兩小時。祝你有個愉快的旅程。）

M: Thank you. Bye.（M: 謝謝妳，再見。）

25. The man was going to fly to <u>Thailand</u>.
    那個男人將飛往<u>泰國</u>。

26. The man wanted the flight on the date of <u>Feb. 4th</u>.
    那個男人想要搭<u>二月四日</u>的班機。

27. The number of the flight was <u>2316</u>.
    班機號碼是 <u>2316</u>。

28. The flight was at Gate <u>7</u>, New York City Airport.
    班機是在紐約市機場的 <u>7</u> 登機門。

29. The departure time of the flight was at <u>9:45</u>.
    班機的起飛時間是<u>九點四十五分</u>。

30. The man paid <u>786</u> for the ticket.
    那個男人買機票花了<u>七百八十六元</u>。

全新國中會考英語聽力精選(中)原文及參考答案

Unit 3

I、Listen and choose the right picture. （根據你所聽到的內容，選出相應的圖片。）（6分）

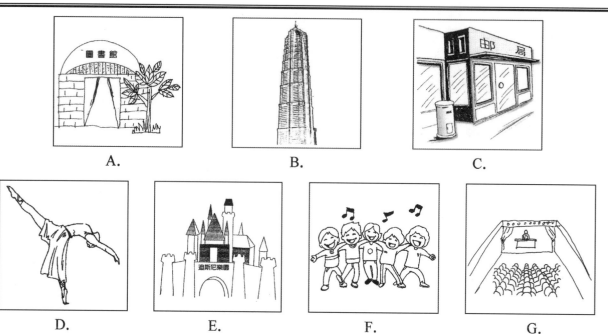

A.　　　　　　　　B.　　　　　　　　C.

D.　　　　　　　　E.　　　　　　　　F.　　　　　　　　G.

1. A new library was built here this year.
   （今年這裡蓋了一個新的圖書館。）
   答案：(A)

2. People go to the post office to post letters.
   （人們去郵局寄信。）
   答案：(C)

3. Jane started learning ballet at the age of seven.
   （Jane 載七歲的時候開始學芭蕾。）
   答案：(D)

4. Sun Flower Middle School is holding an art festival in the hall and five children are singing.
   （Sun Flower 中學在禮堂舉辦藝術季，五個兒童正在唱歌。）
   答案：(F)

5. Is there a Disneyland Park in Shanghai?
   （上海有迪士尼公園嗎？）

答案：(E)

6. There is a big meeting room in our school.
   （我們學校有一個大型會議室。）
   答案：(G)

II、Listen and choose the best response to the sentence you hear.（根據你所聽到的句子，選出最恰當的應答句。）（6分）

---

7. What's your father like?
   （你的父親長得怎樣？）
   (A)He is handsome.（他很帥。）
   (B)He is watering the flowers.（他在澆花。）
   (C)He likes reading.（他喜歡閱讀。）
   (D)He is kind and friendly.（他和藹可親也很友善。）
   答案：(A)

8. Could you show me how to use this calculator?
   （你能告訴我怎麼用這個計算機嗎？）
   (A)That's right.（對。）
   (B)I'm right.（我是對的。）
   (C)All right.（好。）
   (D)That's all right.（沒關係。）
   答案：(C)

9. What can we use a vacuum cleaner to do?
   （我們能用吸塵器做甚麼事？）
   (A)To wash clothes.（洗衣服。）
   (B)To wash dishes.（洗盤子。）
   (C)To clean houses.（清掃房子。）
   (D)To make the air clean.（讓空氣乾淨。）
   答案：(C)

10. I hope our country will become more and more beautiful.
    （我希望我們的國家會變得越來越漂亮。）
    (A)I think so.（我也這麼認為。）
    (B)No, I don't think so.（不，我不認為如此。）
    (C)I hope not.（我不希望。）

(D)I hope so.（我也希望。）

答案：(D)

11. I wasn't able to make a homepage before the New Year's Day.
（新年前，我做不了一個網頁。）

(A)So was I.（我也行。）

(B)Neither was I.（我也不行。）

(C)So do I.（我也能。）

(D)Neither do I.（我也不能。）

答案：(B)

12. You really played well during the basketball game.
（你在籃球賽中打得真好。）

(A)Are you kidding?（你在開玩笑嗎？）

(B)No, of course not.（不，當然不。）

(C)Thank you.（謝謝你。）

(D)Congratulations.（恭喜。）

答案：(C)

Ⅲ、Listen to the dialogue and choose the best answer to the question you hear.（根據你所聽到的對話和問題，選出最恰當的答案。）（6分）

13. M: Mum. I'm so sorry that I only had got 60 in this English test.
（M: 媽，很抱歉我的英文考試只得了六十分。）

W: Don't worry, my dear. Try your best and work harder next time.
（W: 親愛的，別擔心。下次盡你所能，多努力一點。）

M: Thank you.
（M: 謝謝你。）

Question: How's the boy's mother?
（問題：男孩的母親怎麼樣？）

(A)She is beautiful.（她很美麗。）

(B)She is kind.（她很和善。）

(C)She loses her temper easily.（她很容易生氣。）

(D)She never scolds her son.（她從不責備她的兒子。）

答案：(B)

14. W: Sue can read 210 pages in an hour.
（W: Sue 一個小時可以讀兩百一十頁。）

M: So can I. What about you, Linda?
（M: 我也可以。Linda，你呢？）

W: I can read a little bit faster than you and Sue. I can read 4 pages a minute.
（W: 我可以讀得比你跟 Sue 快一點點。我一分鐘可以讀四頁。）

Question: How many pages can Linda read in half an hour?
（問題：Linda 半小時可以讀幾頁？）

(A)210 pages.（210 頁。）

(B)4 pages.（4 頁。）

(C)240 pages.（240 頁。）

(D)120 pages.（120 頁。）

答案：(D)

15. W: Jerry, did Tom go to attend the meeting last Thursday?
（W: Jerry，Tom 上星期四去參加會議了嗎？）

M: No, he didn't. He had got a high fever.
（M: 不，他沒去。他發高燒。）

W: Then you went there, didn't you?
（W: 你去了，對嗎？）

M: No. I asked Sam to attend the meeting instead.
（M: 沒去。我另外請 Sam 參加會議。）

Question: Who attended the meeting last Thursday?
（問題：誰參加了上星期四的會議？）

(A)Jerry.

(B)Tom.

(C)Sam.

(D)Jim.

答案：(C)

16. W: Hello, how are you?
（W: 哈囉，你好嗎？）

M: I'm very well. How was your life in Dalian?
（M: 我很好。你在大連的生活怎麼樣？）

W: Very good, thank you. But it rained a lot. I had to take an umbrella with me almost every day. What was the weather like in Hangzhou?
（W: 非常好，謝謝你。但是那兒常下雨。我幾乎每天都要帶雨傘。杭州的天氣怎麼樣呢？）

M: Oh, it was very hot and sunny. The sun was very bright and the wind was very weak.

（M: 喔，天氣晴朗，非常炎熱。太陽很亮，風很小。）

Question: What was the weather like in Dalian?

（問題：大連的天氣怎麼樣？）

(A)Rainy. （多雨的。）

(B)Sunny. （晴朗的。）

(C)Hot. （炎熱的。）

(D)Windy. （有風的。）

答案：(A)

17. W: The pop music concert started at 7.30, didn't it, Tom?

（W: Tom，流行音樂的音樂會在七點半開始，對不對？）

M: Yes. I got to the stadium at 7.15.

（M: 是的。我七點十五分到達體育館。）

W: What about Linda?

（W: Linda 呢？）

M: She got there 5 minutes earlier than me.

（M: 他比我早五分鐘到。）

Question: When did Linda arrive at the stadium?

（問題：Linda 何時抵達體育館？）

(A)7.30. （七點三十分。）

(B)7.15. （七點十五分。）

(C)7.10. （七點十分。）

(D)7.20. （七點二十分。）

答案：(C)

18. W: Is it serious, Doctor Smith?

（W: Smith 醫生，嚴重嗎？）

M: Not really. It's just a cold. Take this medicine, drink more water and you'll be all right soon.

（M: 不嚴重。只是感冒。吃藥、多喝水，你很快就會好了。）

Question: Where are they talking?

（問題：他們在哪裡談話？）

(A)In the office. （在辦公室。）

(B)In a hospital. （在醫院。）

(C)At a bus stop.（在公車站。）

(D)In a supermarket.（在超級市場。）

答案：(B)

Ⅳ、Listen to the passage and decide whether the following statements are True (T) or False (F).（判斷下列句子內容是否符合你所聽到的短文內容，符合的用"T"表示，不符合的用"F"表示。）（6分）

Good afternoon, boys and girls.

（午安，男孩們、女孩們。）

I have something to tell you.

（我有些事要告訴你們。）

We're going to do some cleaning after school.

（我們放學後要做一些清掃工作。）

The radio says it will be windy at night, so please remember to close the doors and windows when you leave.

（收音機說晚上的風會很大，所以請記得離開時關上門窗。）

The temperature will fall below zero tomorrow morning.

（明天早晨的氣溫會下降到零度以下。）

Please don't forget to put on more clothes.

（請不要忘記多穿衣服。）

Mr. Wang is away today.

（Wang 先生今天請假。）

He is ill and in hospital.

（他生病了，住院。）

I hope you can go to see him.

（我希望妳們可以去看看他。）

But you don't need to buy him anything.

（但是你們不需要買東西給他。）

By the way, there's a lot of homework this evening.

（另外，今天晚上有許多功課。）

You must finish doing it and bring it to school tomorrow morning.

（你們要寫完，並且在明天早上帶來學校。）

You'd better not watch TV till too late.

（你們電視最好不要看得太晚。）

Now let's begin our cleaning.

（現在讓我們開始清掃工作吧。）

19. We're going to have a rest.
（我們將休息一下。）

答案：（F錯）

20. It will rain at night.
（晚上會下雨。）

答案：（F錯）

21. The temperature will fall below zero tomorrow morning.
（明天早上的氣溫會下降到零度以下。）

答案：（T對）

22. Mr Wang is in hospital.
（Wang 先生在醫院。）

答案：（T對）

23. Students can watch TV until very late today.
（今天學生們可以看電視看到很晚。）

答案：（F錯）

24. The students are going to clean their classroom soon.
（學生們馬上就要清掃他們的教室。）

答案：（T對）

Ⅴ、Listen and fill in the blanks.（根據你所聽到的內容，用適當的單詞完成下面的句子。每空格限填一詞。）（6分）

Hello, my name is John.
（哈囉，我的名字是 John。）
I'm a big boy.
（我是一個大男孩。）
I'm twelve.
（我十二歲。）
I weigh fifty-two kilograms, but I'm only a hundred and five centimeters tall.
（我重五十二公斤，但是我只有一百零五公分高。）
My mother is worried about me.
（我母親很擔心我。）
She took me to see the doctor, Mrs. White.
（她帶我去看醫生，White 小姐。）
I told her my favorite food is fried chicken, chocolate and ice cream.
（我告訴她我最愛的食物是炸雞、巧克力和冰淇淋。）

（我跟她說我最喜歡的食物是炸雞、巧克力和冰淇淋。）

I don't like fruit or vegetables.

（我不喜歡水果和蔬菜。）

I like playing video games and watching TV at home for a long time.

（我喜歡長時間在家打電玩和看電視。）

I hate doing exercise.

（我討厭運動。）

The doctor examined me and said I was overweight and I was not healthy because I had a bad diet.

（醫生為我做了檢查，她說，因為我的飲食習慣不好，所以我超重而且很不健康。）

She told me to do more exercise, eat more fruit and vegetables, and I would be thinner and healthier.

（她要我多做運動，吃多一點蔬菜和水果，這樣我就會越來越瘦、越來越健康。）

● John is 12 years old and __25__ centimeters tall.

（John 十二歲，____公分高。）

● His favourite food is fried chicken, __26__ and ice cream.

（他最喜歡的食物是炸雞，____和冰淇淋。）

● He likes playing video games and __27__ TV for a long time.

（他喜歡長時間玩電玩和____電視。）

● The doctor thinks that he is not very __28__ and he is __29__.

（醫生認為他不是很____而且____。）

● The doctor also thinks that John has a bad diet and needs to do more __30__ and eat more fruit and vegetables.

（醫生也認為 John 有不好的飲食習慣，而且需要做更多____，吃更多水果和蔬菜。）

25. 答案：105

26. 答案：Chocolate (巧克力)

27. 答案：watching (觀看)

28. 答案：healthy (健康的)

29. 答案：overweight (過重)

30. 答案：exercise (運動)

Unit 4

I、**Listen and choose the right picture.**

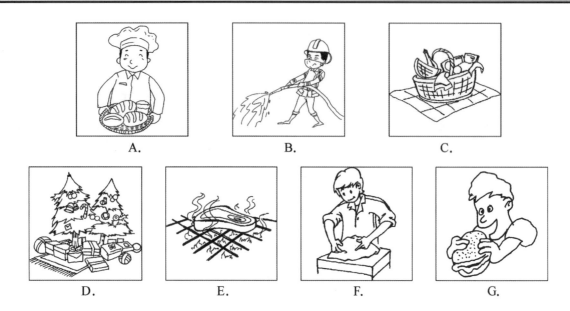

1. Mum has put so many decorations on the Christmas tree. It looks very beautiful.
   (媽媽在聖誕樹上放了很多裝飾品。它看起來很漂亮。)
   答案：(D)

2. I'm full. I can't eat up the hamburger. (我吃飽了。我無法吃完這個漢堡。)
   答案：(G)

3. Barbecued meat tastes nice with honey. (烤肉加蜂蜜很好吃。)
   答案：(E)

4. Jackie works as a baker and bakes very nice cakes.
   (傑基的工作是烘焙師並且烘焙出很好的蛋糕。)
   答案：(A)

5. Ben tries to make the flour into a dough. (班試著把麵粉製成麵團。)
   答案：(F)

6. My sister has prepared a big basket of fruits for the picnic.
   (我的姊妹為了野餐準備了一大籃的水果。)
   答案：(C)

II、**Listen to the dialogue and choose the best answer to the question you hear.**

7. W: When does the shop open in the morning? (女：這間商店早上幾點開門？)
   M: It opens at 9 a.m. (男：它上午九點開。)

W: How long is it open? (女：它營業時間多長？)

W: It's open till 6 p.m. on weekdays and till 8 p.m. at weekends.

(男：在週間它營業到下午六點而週末則到晚上八點。)

Question: How long is the shop open on Saturday? (問題：此商店星期六營業時間多長？)

(A)For 11 hours. (十一個小時)　　　　(B)For 9 hours. (九個小時)

(C)For 10 hours. (十個小時)　　　　(D)For 8 hours. (八個小時)

答案：(A)

8.　W: Dennis, how long have you been in China? (女：丹尼斯，你在中國待多久了？)

M: I stayed in Guangzhou for two weeks and in Shanghai for another week. I will go back in two weeks. (男：我在廣州停留了兩星期而在上海又一星期。我還有兩星期就要回去了。)

Question: How many weeks will Dennis stay in China?

(問題：丹尼斯將在中國停留多少星期？)

(A)For 6 weeks. (六個星期)　　　　(B)For 5 weeks. (五個星期)

(C)For 4 weeks. (四個星期)　　　　(D)For 3 weeks. (三個星期)

答案：(B)

9.　W: What are you doing, Bob? (女：你在做什麼，包伯？)

M: I'm busy packing. The plane will take off in an hour and a half. There is only a little time for me to catch it. (男：我忙著收拾行李。班機將在一個半小時後起飛。我只剩一點點時間趕飛機。)

W: Can I help you? (女：我能幫你嗎？)

M: It's all right, thanks. Let me manage it myself. (男：沒關係啦，謝謝。讓我自己搞定。)

Question: What is Bob doing now? (問題：包伯現在正在做什麼？)

(A)He's taking off his shoes. (他正在脫鞋子。)

(B)He's managing. (他正在處理。)

(C)He's catching the plane. (他正在趕飛機。)

(D)He's packing. (他在收拾行李。)

答案：(D)

10.　W: Long time no see. You seem to be about twenty years old. You were just a kid when I left.

(女：好久不見。你看起來大約二十歲。當我離開的時候你只是個小孩子。)

M: Yes. I was only thirteen years old when you left home nine years ago.

(男：對。當你九年前離開家時我才十三歲。)

Question: How old is the young man? (問題：這位年輕男士幾歲？)

(A)20 years old. (二十歲)　　　　(B)22 years old. (二十二歲)

(C)29 years old. (二十九歲)　　　　(D)30 years old. (三十歲)

答案：(B)

11.　W: I'm looking for a pair of brown shoes. (女：我正在找一雙褐色的鞋子。)

M: Sorry, we haven't got brown shoes. But would you like to try on this pair of black shoes? They are very comfortable to wear.

（男：抱歉，我們沒有褐色的鞋子。但妳想要試穿這雙黑色的鞋子嗎？穿起來很舒適。）

Question: Where does this conversation take place? （問題：這段對話在哪裡發生？）

(A)At home. (在家裡)　　　　　　　　　(B)At her friend's home. (在她的朋友家)

(C)At his friend's home. (在他的朋友家)　(D)At a shop. (在一間商店)

答案：(D)

12. W: Good evening. My name is Helen. I booked a table by phone two days ago.

（女：晚安。我的名字是海倫。我兩天前以電話預約了一桌。）

M: Please wait a moment. Let me check it for you. Is it the table with ten seats?

（男：請等一下。讓我為您查一查。是一張十位的桌子嗎？）

W: That's right. (女：是的。)

M: OK. This way, please. (男：好。這邊請。)

Question: Where does the conversation probably take place?

（問題：這段對話可能是在哪裡發生？）

(A)In a hotel. (在旅館)　　　　　　　　(B)In a supermarket. (在超市)

(C)In a restaurant. (在一間餐廳)　　　　(D)At a cinema. (在電影院)

答案：(C)

13. W: It's very strange that our daughter stayed at home the day before yesterday. She usually goes out for fun on Sundays.

（女：很奇怪，我們的女兒前天待在家裡。星期天她通常會出去找樂子。）

M: She stayed at home in order to wait for a friend. She had a date with the friend of hers. She wanted to ask her for help.

（男：她待在家裡為了等一個朋友。她和她那個朋友有約。她想要找她幫忙。）

Question: What day is it? （問題：今天星期幾？）

(A)Tuesday. (星期二)　　　　　　　　　(B)Sunday. (星期天)

(C)Monday. (星期一)　　　　　　　　　　　　　　(D)Saturday. （星期六）

答案：(A)

14. W: Excuse me, could you please tell me how to get to Shanghai Railway Station?

（女：不好意思，可否請您告訴我怎麼去上海火車站？）

M: Take the second turning on the left. Then walk on to the end of the road. It's fifteen minutes' walk. Take the No.30 bus there. It will take you thirty-five more minutes to get there.

（男：在左邊第二個街口左轉。然後走到那條路的盡頭。這段路要走十五分鐘。在那裡搭三十路巴士。到那裡妳需要再花三十五分鐘。）

Question: How long will it take the woman to get to Shanghai Railway Station?

（問題：去上海火車站將要花這位女士多少時間？）

(A)45 minutes. (四十五分鐘)　　　　　(B)50 minutes. (五十分鐘)

(C)40 minutes. (四十分鐘)　　　　　　(D)55 minutes. (五十五分鐘)

答案：(B)

15. M: Can you complete the form in five minutes? (男：您可以在五分鐘內填完此表格嗎？)

    W: Sorry. I have a phone call to answer now. (女：抱歉。我現在有通電話要接聽。)

    Question: The woman can't fill in the form now, can she?

    (問題：這位女士現在不能填寫此表格，是嗎？)

    (A)Yes, she can. (是的，她能。)　　　　　(B)Yes, she can't. (是的，她不能。)

    (C)No, she can. (不，她能。)　　　　　　(D)No, she can't. (不，她不能。)

    答案：(D)

16. W: Would you like to attend the lecture given by Dr. Chen?

    （女：你會想出席陳博士主講的講座嗎？）

    M: I'd love to. When will it begin? (男：我很想去。它幾時開始？)

    W: At 1 p.m. I'm afraid we have to hurry. (女：下午一點。我恐怕我們得趕快。)

    M: Come on. There is still plenty of time. We have three quarters to get there.

    （男：拜託ㄟ。還有很多時間。我們有四十五分鐘時間。）

    Question: What time is it now? (問題：現在幾點？)

    (A)12.00 noon. (中午十二點)　　　　　(B)12.15 p.m. (下午十二點十五分)

    (C)11.45 a.m. (上午十一點四十五分)　　(D)12.30 p.m. (下午十二點半)

    答案：(B)

Ⅲ、Listen to the passage and decide whether the following statements are True (T) or False (F).

I have had a great time travelling the world, and have learnt a lot about the eating habits of people in different countries.

我在世界各地旅遊很快樂，而且了解到很多不同國家人們的飲食習慣。

In China, for example, people use chopsticks to eat with. They have eaten this way for thousands of years, but I found chopsticks very difficult to use. Chinese cooks usually cut the food into small pieces, and put each dish on a different plate. At dinner, everyone sits at a round table. The hostess puts the dishes of food in the middle of the table, and everyone helps themselves with chopsticks or spoons. In Shanghai, I saw people eat chicken's feet and smelly tofu. I have not seen this kind of food in the UK.

例如，在中國，人們用筷子吃東西。他們以這種方法吃東西幾千年了，但我發現筷子很難用。中國廚師通常把食物切成小塊，然後把各道菜盛放在不同的盤子上。晚餐時，每個人坐在圓桌旁。女主人把一盤盤的菜放在桌子中間，每個人用筷子或湯匙自行取用。在上海，我看到人們吃雞爪和臭豆腐。我在英國沒有看過這類食物。

In Japan, people also use chopsticks, but each person has a separate tray of food. Each tray has several small dishes and bowls of food on it. The people at a table usually do not get food from plates in the middle of the table. The most famous Japanese food is sashimi — raw fish. I found it very delicious.

在日本，人們也用筷子，但是每個人有各別一托盤的食物。每個托盤上有數小碟和數碗食物。同桌的人們通常不會從桌子中間的盤子上取用食物。最有名的日本料理是刺身－生魚。我發現它很好吃。

In the UK, people usually use a knife and fork. For a family dinner, the mother or father will put the food in the middle of the table. Everyone passes the food around. As they pass the food, they take some and put it on their plates. They often eat food like roast beef and potatoes. The father will cut off a large piece of roast beef and put it on each person's plate. They use their knives to cut the food, and their fork to eat it.

在英國,人們通常用刀叉。家族的晚餐,母親或父親會把食物放在桌子中間。每個人傳遞食物一圈。當他們傳遞食物時,他們取用一些然後把它放在自己的盤子上。他們通常吃烤牛肉和馬鈴薯這樣的食物。父親會切下大塊的烤牛肉然後放到每個人的盤子上。他們用他們的刀子切割食物,用他們的叉子來吃。

17. People in China do not use spoons. (在中國的人們不使用湯匙。)
    答案:(F錯)

18. Some people have trouble using chopsticks. (有些人在使用筷子上有困難。)
    答案:(T對)

19. People in the UK do not usually eat chicken's feet or smelly tofu.
    (在英國的人們不常吃雞爪或臭豆腐。)
    答案:(T對)

20. In Japan, people help themselves from plates of food in the middle of the table.
    (在日本,人們從餐桌中間的一盤盤料理自行取用。)
    答案:(F錯)

21. Most people in the UK use chopsticks. (大多數在英國的人使用筷子。)
    答案:(F錯)

22. In the UK, the cook cuts all the food into small pieces. (在英國,廚師把所有食物切成小塊。)
    答案:(F錯)

23. In the UK, people help themselves to the food. (在英國,人們自行取用料理。)
    答案:(F錯)

IV、Listen to the dialogue and fill in the blanks.

Mr Brown: Marry, are you in a hurry? (布朗先生:瑪莉,妳在趕時間嗎?)

Mary: Yes, I am. Please excuse me, Mr Brown. I must run to the shops to buy some fruit and soya sauce or I shall be late for school.

瑪莉:對,我是。不好意思,布朗先生。我必須跑去店裡買些水果和醬油否則我上學將會遲到。

Mr Brown: Why doesn't your mother do the shopping herself?

布朗先生:為何妳母親不自己採購?

Mary: She is ill. She hasn't eaten any bread or meat since Sunday. She hasn't slept well for two nights.

瑪莉：她生病了。她自從星期天起就沒有吃任何麵包或肉。她兩個晚上都沒有睡好。

Mr Brown: Have you given her some chicken soup? (布朗先生：妳有給她一些雞湯嗎？)

Mary: I've just been to the shop for a chicken, but Mum won't be able to drink the soup. She's very tired all the time. She doesn't want to eat anything. We don't know what to do. We've tried everything.

瑪莉：我剛剛才去店裡買了一隻雞，但我媽無法喝湯。她總是很疲倦。她不想吃任何東西。我們不知道該怎麼辦。我們什麼都試過了。

Mr Brown: Have you asked her to drink some orange juice?

布朗先生：妳有要求她喝一些柳橙汁嗎？

Mary: Yes! I have asked her to drink some orange juice. I guess it is good for her health. I have to go now. See you, Mr Brown.

瑪莉：有！我有要求她喝一些柳橙汁。我猜那對她的健康有益。我現在必須走了。再見，布朗先生。

What has Mary done? (瑪莉做了些什麼？)
- She has tried to get her mother to have some __24__ and __25__
  (她試著讓她母親吃些麵包和肉。)
- She has asked her mother to have some __26__ soup
  (她要求她母親喝些雞湯。)
- She has asked her mother to drink some __27__ juice
  (她要求她母親喝些柳橙汁。)

What hasn't Mary's mother done? (瑪莉的母親沒有做什麼？)
- She hasn't eaten anything since __28__
  (她自從星期天起就沒吃任何東西。)
- She hasn't __29__ well for __30__ nights
  (她兩個晚上沒睡好。)

24. 答案：bread (麵包)

25. 答案：meat (肉)

26. 答案：chicken (雞)

27. 答案：orange (柳橙)

28. 答案：Sunday (星期天)

29. 答案：slept (睡)

30. 答案：two/2 (二)

Unit 5

Ⅰ、Listen and choose the right picture.（根據你所聽到的內容，選出相應的圖片。）（6分）

A.   B.   C.

D.   E.   F.   G.

1. I seldom watch television with my cousins. But yesterday we sat together and watched a very interesting cartoon.
   (我很少跟我表姊弟一起看電視。但是昨天我們坐在一起看了一部很有趣的卡通。)
   答案：(E)

2. Look at Susan! She has fallen asleep but the book is still in her hand.
   (看看 Susan！雖然她睡著了但是書還在她手上。)
   答案：(A)

3. Do people still learn English on the radio today? I know that Teddy does.
   (現在人們依然聽收音機學英文嗎？我知道 Teddy 是這樣的。)
   答案：(B)

4. Have a look at the newspaper. There is an important news report today!
   (看一下報紙。今天有一則非常重要的新聞報導！)
   答案：(C)

5. Some children are making sandcastles on the beach now.
   (一些孩子現在在海邊堆沙堡。)
   答案：(F)

6. Henry laughed happily because he had sent his model plane into the air successfully.
   (Henry 笑得好開心，因為他成功地將他的模型飛機送上天空。)
   答案：(D)

7.　W: Tom, can you tell me where the museum is? (W: Tom，你能告訴我博物館在哪裡嗎？)

M: It's far from here. (M: 那離這裡很遠。)

W: Can I take a bus there? (W: 我能搭公車去那裡嗎？)

M: I'm not sure which bus gets there, but you can go there by bike.
(M: 我不確定哪一班公車會到，但是你可以騎腳踏車去那兒。)

W: How long will it take me to get there by bike? (W: 騎腳踏車要花多久時間呢？)

M: About twenty minutes. (M: 差不多二十分鐘。)

W: Thank you for your advice. (W: 謝謝你的建議。)

Question: How will the girl probably go to the museum?

(問題：那女孩大概會怎麼去博物館？)

(A)On foot. (走路。)　　　　　　　　　(B)By bus. (搭公車。)

(C)By bike. (騎腳踏車。)　　　(D)By taxi. (搭計程車。)

答案：(C)

8.　M: Let's hurry, or we'll be late for the film.
(M: 我們要快一點，要不然我們看電影就要遲到了。)

W: What time is it now? (W: 現在幾點？)

M: It's 2.00 now. There are only twenty minutes left. (M: 現在兩點。只剩下二十分了。)

W: OK. Shall we take a taxi there? It will take us only five minutes to get there.
(W: 好。我們搭計程車去那兒好嗎？我們只要花五分鐘就到了。)

M: But it's expensive. Let's take a bus there. It'll take us about ten minutes.
(M: 但是那很貴。我們搭公車去吧。大概十分鐘。)

W: All right. (W: 好。)

Question: When does the film begin? (問題：電影幾點開始？)

(A)At 2.00. （兩點。）　　　　　(B)At 2.05. （兩點五分。）

(C)At 2.10. （兩點十分。）　　　(D)At 2.20. (兩點二十分。)

答案：(D)

9.　M: What can I do for you? (M: 我能為你服務嗎？)

W: I'm looking for a coat for my son. (W: 我想為我兒子找一件外套。)

M: We have all kinds and sizes of coats. Which one would you like?
(M: 我們有各種款式與尺寸的外套。你想要哪一種？)

W: My son is only a child. I don't want any expensive one.
(W: 我兒子只是個小孩。我不想要太貴的。)

M: I see. This one is 50 dollars, and that one is only 25 dollars.

(M: 我知道了。這件 50 元，那件只要 25 元。)

W: Can I take two with 40 dollars? (W: 我以 40 元買兩件可以嗎？)

Question: How much does the woman want to pay for each coat?

(問題：每一件外套每那女人想花多少錢？)

(A)100 dollars. (100 元)　　　　　　　(B)50 dollars. (50 元)

(C)25 dollars. (25 元)　　　　　　　　　　　　(D)20 dollars. (20 元)

答案：(D)

10. W: Where did you go yesterday? (W: 你昨天去哪兒了？)

　　M: We went to the countryside for a picnic. (M: 我們去鄉下野餐。)

　　W: How about the outing? (W: 這趟郊遊如何？)

　　M: Wonderful. The weather was fine and the air was fresh. (M: 非常棒。天氣好，空氣新鮮。)

　　W: Did your teachers go with you? (W: 你們的老師跟你們一起去嗎？)

　　M: Yes. We all went there except my deskmate Mike.

　　　　(M: 是的。除了我同桌的 Mike 以外我們都去了。)

　　W: I'm sure you must have had a good time. (W: 我相信你們一定玩得很開心。)

　　Question: Who didn't go for the picnic? (問題：誰沒去野餐？)

　　(A)Some students. (一些學生。)　　　　(B)One student. (一位學生。)

　　(C)Some teachers. (一些老師。)　　　　(D)One teacher. (一位老師。)

　　答案：(B)

11. W: Hi, Tom. Why do you look unhappy? (W: 嗨，Tom。你為什麼看起來不開心？)

　　M: We had a maths exam just now. I didn't do it well. (M: 我們剛剛考完數學。我考得不好。)

　　W: But how do you know it? (W: 但是你怎麼知道呢？)

　　M: Some classmates' answers are different from mine. (M: 有些同學的答案和我的不一樣。)

　　W: Don't worry. Maybe theirs are wrong. (W: 別擔心。或許他們是錯的。)

　　Question: What does Tom think of his exam? (問題：Tom 覺得他的考試怎麼樣？)

　　(A)Terrible. (很糟。)　　　　　　　　(B)Just so-so. (普通。)

　　(C)Well done. (很好。)　　　　　　　　(D)The best. (最好的。)

　　答案：(A)

12. W: Where is Mary? (W: Mary 在哪兒？)

　　M: She's at home, I think. We've asked her to go to the cinema, but she won't go with us.

　　　　(M: 我想她在家。我們找她去看電影，但是她不跟我們去。)

　　W: Why not? (W: 為什麼不去？)

　　M: She says she's seen the film twice. (M: 她說那部電影她看過兩次了。)

W: What's she going to do then? (W: 那麼她要做甚麼？)

M: She is going to stay at home, watching TV. (M: 她要待在家看電視。)

Question: Why doesn't Mary go to the cinema? (問題：為什麼 Mary 不去看電影？)

(A)She doesn't like the film. (她不喜歡那部電影。)

(B)She has seen the film. (她已經看過那部電影。)

(C)She'd like to stay at home. (她想待在家。)

(D)She likes watching TV. (她喜歡看電視。)

答案：(B)

13. W: Excuse me, does this bus go to Shanghai Library?

(W: 不好意思，這班公車去上海圖書館嗎？)

M: Yes, it does. (W: 是的。)

W: Where shall I get off? (W: 我該在哪裡下車？)

M: At Huaihai Road. (M: 在 Huaihai 路。)

W: Thank you very much. (W: 非常謝謝你。)

M: You are welcome. (M: 不客氣。)

Question: Where are they talking? (問題：他們在哪裡談話？)

(A)In Shanghai Library. (在上海圖書館。)

(B)On Huaihai Road. (在 Huaihai 路上。)

(C)On the bus. (在公車上。)

(D)On the underground. (在地鐵上。)

答案：(C)

14. W: Could you say something about yourself? (W: 你能談談你自己嗎？)

M: OK. I left college at the age of 22. Three years later, I was sent to Shanghai.

(M: 好。我二十二歲的時候離開了學校。三年後，我被派到上海。)

W: That's in the year of 2002. (W: 那是在 2002 年。)

M: No, I came to China in 2001. (M: 不，我 2001 年來中國。)

W: So you have been here for a long time. (W: 所以你在這裡已經很長時間了。)

M: That's right. (M: 沒錯。)

Question: When did the man leave college? (問題：那男人何時離開學校？)

(A)In 1998. (1998 年)　　　　(B)In 1999. (1999 年)

(C)In 2000. (2000 年)　　　　(D)In 2001. (2001 年)

答案：(A)

15. M: Would you like to have a cigarette? (M: 你想來根香菸嗎？)

W: No, thanks. I've given up smoking. (W: 不，謝謝。我已經戒菸了。)

M: It's not easy. I've tried many times, but I failed. How can you make it?

(M: 那不容易。我試了好多次但是都失敗了。你怎麼辦到的？)

W: Have you heard an English saying? "Where there is a will, there is a way."

(W: 你聽過一句英文諺語嗎？「Where there is a will, there is a way. (有志者事竟

成)」。)

M: Oh! You have a strong will. You have set a good example to me.

(M: 喔。你有很強的意志力。你已經為我樹立了一個好榜樣。)

Question: Who still smokes? (問題：誰仍然抽菸？)

(A)The man. (那男人。)   (B)The woman. (那女人。)

(C)Both of them. (兩個人。)   (D)Neither of them. (兩個人都不抽。)

答案：(A)

16. W: What's the matter, Mike? You look upset. (W: Mike 你怎麼了？你看起來很沮喪。)

M: I didn't pass the English test. (M: 我沒通過英語測驗。)

W: I think you'd better work still harder. (W: 我想你該更努力用功。)

M: But I'm not interested in it at all. (M: 但是我一點興趣也沒有。)

W: Oh, really? English is an important tool. We must learn it well.

(W: 喔，真的嗎？英文是非常重要的工具。我們必須把它學好。)

Question: Why does Mike look unhappy? (問題：為什麼 Mike 看起來不開心？)

(A)Because he worked hard at English. (因為他努力讀英文。)

(B)Because he is not interested in English. (因為他對英文沒興趣。)

(C)Because he didn't pass the Chinese test. (因為他沒通過中文測驗。)

(D)Because he failed in the English test. (因為他英語測驗不及格。)

答案：(D)

Ⅲ、Listen to the passage and decide whether the following statements are True (T) or False (F). (判斷下列句子是否符合你所聽到的短文內容，符合的用 T 表示，不符合的用 F 表示。)(7分)

Jean Champollion （1790~1832） was very good at languages. He learnt twelve languages in his life. When he was eighteen, he began teaching history at university. He was younger than many of his students!

Jean Champollion （1790~1832）非常擅長語言。他一生中學了十二種語言。在他十八歲的時候，他開始在大學教歷史。他比許多學生還年輕！

Jean was very interested in ancient Egypt and in 1821 he began to study the Rosetta Stone. A group of soldiers found this stone at Rosetta when Jean was still a young boy. It was under the sand for hundreds of years before they dug it up. There was a lot of strange writing on the stone. The writing was in three languages. One of the languages was ancient Egyptian. No one could read it at that time. But Jean worked out its secret.

Jean 對古埃及非常感興趣，1821 年，他開始研讀「羅賽塔石碑(Rosetta Stone)」。當 Jean 還是個年輕男孩的時候，一群士兵在羅賽塔發現了這塊石碑。在他們把它挖掘出來以前，它已經在沙地底下好幾百年了。石碑上有很多奇怪的文字。這段文字以三種語言寫成。其中一種語言是古埃及文。那時候沒人能讀埃及文。但是 Jean 解出它的秘密。

Ancient Egyptian was not a language with letters and words like English. It was full of signs. According to many experts, these signs showed things and ideas. Jean did not completely agree. He thought that some of them showed sounds. He found fifteen signs of this kind in his study of the Rosetta Stone. Today, it is possible to understand ancient Egyptian from 4,000 years ago because of Jean's discovery.

古埃及文不像英文這種語言有著字母和單字。它充滿了符號。根據許多專家的說法，這些符號表示了事物和想法。Jean 完全不同意。他認為有些符號代表聲音。他在他的「羅賽塔石碑(Rosetta Stone)」研究中發現了十五種這樣的符號。因為 Jean 的發現，我們現在才可能了解四千年前的古埃及文。

17. Jean Champollion learned about twenty languages in his life.
    (Jean Champolliony 在他的一生中學了約二十種語言。)
    答案：(F 錯)

18. Jean became very interested in ancient Egypt when he was young.
    (Jean 年輕的時候對古埃及非常感興趣。)
    答案：(T 對)

19. Jean started to study the Rosetta Stone in 1921. (Jean 在 1921 年開始研究羅賽塔石碑。)
    答案：(F 錯)

20. Some scientists found the Rosetta Stone under the sand when Jean was a small boy.
    (當 Jean 是個小男孩的時候，一些科學家發現在沙地底下發現羅賽塔石碑。)
    答案：(F 錯)

21. There was a lot of strange writing on the stone. (石碑上有許多奇怪的文字。)
    答案：(T 對)

22. Ancient Egyptian was a language with letters and words like English.
    (古埃及文是一種像英語一樣有字母與單字的語言。)
    答案：(F 錯)

23. Jean thought that some of the signs on the Rosetta Stone told about sounds.
    (Jean 認為羅賽塔石碑上的一些符號表述了聲音。)
    答案：(T 對)

IV、Listen to the dialogue and fill in the blanks. (根據你聽到的對話，完成下列內容，每空格限填一詞。)(7 分)

Sun Fei: Hi, Sally. I have some problems with my project on the languages of the world. Will you please help me find some information in your encyclopaedia?

(Sun Fei: 嗨，Sally。我的那份有關世界語言的計畫有些問題。你能在你的百科全書裡幫我找些資料嗎？)

Sally: Sure! What do you want to know?

(Sally: 當然！你想知道甚麼？)

Sun Fei: Well, people around the world speak different languages, right? But how many languages are there?

(Sun Fei: 嗯，全世界的人說著不同的語言，對吧？但是有多少種語言呢？)

Sally: Let me see. Well, there are more than six thousand different languages in the world today.

(Sally: 讓我看看。嗯，現在世界上有超過六千種不同的語言。)

Sun Fei: Which language has the most speakers? Chinese?

(Sun Fei: 哪一種語言最多人說？中文？)

Sally: You are right. There are more than one thousand three hundred million speakers of Chinese. English is the second. There are about three hundred and fifty million speakers of English in the world.

(Sally: 你說對了。有超過十三億人說中文。英文排第二。世界上大約有三億五千萬人說英文。)

Sun Fei: How about the other people?

(Sun Fei: 其他的人呢？)

Sally: Of course, many people speak neither Chinese nor English. Some languages have only a few speakers — about 40 or 50. In some places, only the old people still speak their language. Neither the parents nor the children learn the old language. When grandparents die, the language will die, too.

(Sally: 當然，許多人不說中文也不說英文。有些語言只有少數人說，大約四十或五十人。有些地方，只有老人依舊說他們的語言。父母與孩子都不學那種老的語言。當祖父母過世的時候，那種語言也就死亡了。)

Sun Fei: It is interesting to learn about languages. Thank you for your information, Sally. It is very useful for my project.

(Sun Fei: 認識語言很有趣。謝謝你的資訊。Sally 這對我的計劃非常有用。)

Sally: It is my pleasure!

(Sally: 這是我的榮幸！)

- There are more than __24__ different languages in the world. (世界是有超過___種不同的語言。)
- __25__ is the language with the most speakers （more than __26__ speakers）. (___是最多人說的語言，超過____人。)
- __27__ is the second （more than __28__ speakers）. ___ 排第二。(超過___人。)
- Some languages have a few speakers—about 40 or __29__. (一些語言只有少數人說，大約四十或____人。)
- Some languages __30__ when grandparents pass away. (當祖父母輩過世的時候，一些語言也___。)

24. 答案：6,000 (六千)
25. 答案：Chinese (中文)
26. 答案：1,300,000,000 (十三億)

27. 答案：English (英文)
28. 答案：350,000,000 (三億五千萬)
29. 答案：50
30. 答案：die (死亡)

全新國中會考英語聽力精選(中)原文及參考答案

Unit 6

I、Listen and choose the right picture.（根據你所聽到的內容，選出相應的圖片。）（6分）

A.　　B.　　C.

D.　　E.　　F.　　G.

1.　I live quite near my school, so I usually get up at 7 o'clock in the morning.
（我住的離我學校相當近，所以我通常早上七點起床。）
答案：(B)

2.　Simon can hear the birds singing in the trees.
（Simon 可以聽見樹上的小鳥在唱歌。）
答案：(D)

3.　When autumn comes, my family usually go on picnics in the countryside.
（當秋天來臨的時候，我家常常去鄉下野餐。）
答案：(C)

4.　When I was young, I usually went to the beach and made sandcastles with my cousin.
（當我年輕的時候，我常常和我表哥去海灘做沙堡。）
答案：(G)

5.　When I lived in the suburbs, I liked watching the beautiful stars at night with my cousin.
（當我住在郊區的時候，我喜歡在晚上和我表姊一起看美麗的星星。）
答案：(A)

6. I have moved to the suburbs, so I have to get up early and go to school by bus.
    （我已經搬到郊區了，所以我必須早起搭公車上學。）
    答案：(E)

II、Listen and choose the best response to the sentence you hear.（根據你所聽到的句子，選出最恰當的應答句。）（6分）

---

7. Where shall I put the table?
    （我該把桌子放在哪裡好呢？）
    (A)On the table, please.（請放在桌上。）
    (B)Opposite the sofa, please.（請放在沙發的對面。）
    (C)Take it away, please.（請把它拿走。）
    (D)Bring it in, please.（請帶它進來。）
    答案：(B)

8. Where is Water Bay on the map of Garden City?
    （在 Garden 市的地圖上，Water 灣在哪裡？）
    (A)It's north of the map.（它在地圖的北邊。）
    (B)It's in the north on the map.（地圖上它在北邊。）
    (C)It's on the north of the map.（它在地圖的北邊。）
    (D)It isn't here.（它不在這裡。）
    答案：(B)

9. How long does it take you to go to school from your home every day?
    （你每天從你家去學校要多久時間？）
    (A)Twice a week.（一星期兩次。）
    (B)Two weeks.（兩個星期。）
    (C)About ten minutes.（大約十分鐘。）
    (D)10 o'clock.（十點鐘。）
    答案：(C)

10. Do you live in the city centre or the suburbs?
    （你住在市中心還是郊區？）
    (A)Yes, I do.（是的，我住。）
    (B)No, I don't.（不，我不住。）
    (C)In the suburbs.（在郊區。）
    (D)I can't decide where to live.（我不能決定住哪兒。）

答案：(C)

11. What did Kitty and Ben do when they lived in the city centre?
（當 Kitty 和 Ben 住在市中心的時候，他們常做甚麼事？）

(A)They usually run their dogs at the beach.（它們常去海邊遛狗。）

(B)They watched the beautiful moon and stars at night.
（它們在晚上看漂亮的月亮和星星。）

(C)They will visit the Great Wall in Beijing.
（他們將參觀北京的長城。）

(D)They have already finished their homework.
（他們已經完成他們的功課。）

答案：(B)

12. What season is it in this picture?
（這張照片是在甚麼季節？）

(A)It's February.（二月。）

(B)It's Friday.（星期五。）

(C)It's spring.（春天。）

(D)It's March 3.（三月三日。）

答案：(C)

Ⅲ、Listen to the dialogue and choose the best answer to the question you hear.（根據你所聽到的對話和問題，選出最恰當的答案。）（6分）

13. W: Jack, your grandpa looks so healthy. He is over eighty years old, isn't he?
（W: Jack，你祖父看來好健康。他超過八十歲了，是嗎？）

M: Yes. He never eats bad food and he works in the garden every day.
（M: 是的。他從不吃不好的食物，而且他每天去花園工作。）

Question: Why is Jack's grandpa so healthy?
（問題：為什麼 Jack 的祖父這麼健康？）

(A)Because he is not old.
（因為他不老。）

(B)Because he eats less food.
（因為他吃得不多。）

(C)Because he works every day.
（因為他每天工作。）

(D)Because he eats good food and works every day.
（因為他吃好的食物而且每天工作。）

答案：(D)

14. M: Where can I find a book on Chinese medicine?
（M: 我在哪裡可以找到有關中醫的書？）

W: There is one on the shelf in Dr Black's office.
（W: Black 醫生辦公室的書架上有一本。）

Question: What is the man looking for?
（問題：那個男人在找甚麼？）

(A)An office.（一間辦公室。）

(B)Dr Black.（Black 醫生。）

(C)A book on Chinese medicine.（一本有關中醫的書。）

(D)A shelf.（一個書架。）

答案：(C)

15. W: Where are our children, John?
（W: John，我們的孩子在哪裡？）

M: Tommy is running on the grass with his dog. Helen is sitting under the tree. Jack is playing video games with his classmates Peter and Tim.
（M: Tommy 在草地上溜狗。Helen 坐在樹下。Jack 和他的同學 Peter 與 Tim 在玩電玩。）

Question: How many children has John got?
（問題：John 有幾個孩子？）

(A)Three.（三個。）

(B)Four.（四個。）

(C)Five.（五個。）

(D)Six.（六個。）

答案：(A)

16. M: Hi, Susan. Haven't seen you for a long time.
（M: 嗨，Susan。好久沒看到你了。）

W: I've been to Beijing during my holidays.
（W: 在我的假期期間，我去了北京。）

M: Have you got any friends there?
（M: 你有朋友在那兒嗎？）

W: No. I went to see my parents. They work in a big factory. It is modern and beautiful.
（W: 沒有。我去看我父母。他們在一家大型工廠上班。它非常現代化和漂亮。）

Question: What did Susan do during her holidays?

（問題：Susan 在她的假期期間做了甚麼？）

(A)She went to see her friends.（她去看她的朋友。）

(B)She went to see her parents.（她去看她父母。）

(C)She worked in a modern factory.（她在一家現代化工廠上班。）

(D)She visited a beautiful farm.（她參觀了漂亮的農場。）

答案：(B)

17. W: Why are you in such a hurry?

（W: 為什麼你那麼急？）

M: I'll go to a meeting at Xinhua Cinema this afternoon. It will begin at 2 o'clock.

（M: 我今天下午要去 Xinhua 電影院參加一個會議。他將在兩點開始。）

W: Take it easy. It's only half past one. You'd better take an underground train. The station is just over there.

（W: 放輕鬆。現在才一點半。你最好搭地鐵。車站就在旁邊。）

M: Thank you. Bye!

（M: 謝謝你。再見。）

Question: What is the man going to do this afternoon?

（問題：這位男士下午要做甚麼？）

(A)To go to a meeting.（去參加會議。）

(B)To take the underground.（去搭地鐵。）

(C)To see a film.（去看電影。）

(D)To look for the underground station.（去找地鐵車站。）

答案：(A)

18. M: What's in your hand?

（M: 你手上是甚麼？）

W: A program. There's going to be an English evening at Fudan University this weekend.

（W: 一張節目單。這個周末在復旦大學有一場英語之夜。）

M: Really? That sounds wonderful. I'd like to go, too, but ...

（M: 真的嗎？聽起來很棒。我也很想去，但是...）

W: Don't worry. I can give you a ticket if you want to.

（W: 別擔心。如果你想去我可以給你一張票。）

M: That's very kind of you.

　　（M：你真好。）

Question: What are they going to do this weekend?

　　（問題：他們在這個周末要做甚麼？）

(A)To buy tickets.（買車票。）

(B)To visit Fudan University.（參觀復旦大學。）

(C)To sing English songs.（唱英文歌。）

(D)To attend an English evening.（參加英語之夜。）

答案：(D)

IV、Listen to the passage and decide whether the following statements are True (T) or False (F).（判斷下列句子內容是否符合你所聽到的短文內容，符合的用"T" 表示，不符合的用"F" 表示。)（6分）

Hi! Jack, how are you doing?

（嗨，Jack。你好嗎？）

I'm having a great time in San Diego.

（我在聖地牙哥玩得好開心。）

We went to the Sea World and saw sharks and starfish.

（我們去海洋世界看鯊魚和海星。）

Perhaps I don't have time to post you a card in Los Angeles because we are going to Disneyland and Hollywood there.

（我可能沒時間從洛杉磯寄卡片給你，因為我們要去那裡的迪士尼樂園和好萊塢。）

They are so famous that I can't miss them.

（它們很有名所以我不能錯過它們。）

I will remember to take as many photos as possible.

（我會記得盡量拍很多照片。）

Then I will fly home.

（之後我就會飛回家。）

My holiday will be over on May 16.

（我的假期將在五月十六日結束。）

Our plane will first arrive in Hong Kong, then in Shanghai.

（我們的飛機會先抵達香港，然後是上海。）

So I will have a chance to meet my aunt Judy in Hong Kong.

（所以我將有機會在香港見見我的阿姨 Judy。）

See you soon.（很快會見到你。）

Best wishes（誠摯的祝福）

19. Jack is having a great time in San Diego.
　　（Jack 在聖地牙哥玩得很開心。）
　　答案：（F 錯）

20. Connie is going to Disneyland and Hollywood.
　　（Connie 將去迪士尼樂園和好萊塢。）
　　答案：（T 對）

21. Connie will post Jack a card in Los Angeles.
　　（Connie 將在洛杉磯寄卡片給 Jack。）
　　答案：（F 錯）

22. Connie will go home by air on May 15.
　　（Connie 將在五月十五日搭飛機回家。）
　　答案：（F 錯）

23. The plane will arrive in Shanghai first.
　　（飛機將先抵達上海。）
　　答案：（F 錯）

24. Connie will visit her aunt in Hong Kong.
　　（Connie 將會在香港拜訪她的阿姨。）
　　答案：（T 對）

V、Listen to the dialogue and complete the table.（根據你所聽到的對話內容，用適當的單詞或數字完成下面的表格。每空格限填一詞或數字。）（6分）

M: Good morning, Jolly Estate Agency. Can I help you?
　　（M: 早安，這裡是 Jolly 房屋仲介。我能為你服務嗎？）
W: Yes. I am looking for a new flat for my family.
　　（W: 是的。我想幫我家人找一間新公寓。）
M: Where would you like to live?
　　（M: 你想住在哪裡？）
W: I prefer to live in the suburbs. I am now living in the city centre, close to the underground. There are shops and restaurants near my flat. It is very convenient, but too noisy. I want to move to a quiet place.
　　（W: 我比較喜歡住在郊區。我現在住在市中心，靠近地鐵。我家附近有商店和餐廳。非常方便，但是太吵了。我想搬到安靜的地方。）

M: What kind of flat do you want?
（M: 你想要怎麼樣的公寓？）

W: I'd like a big flat with three bedrooms. I'm living in a two-bedroom flat now. But my mother is coming to stay with us. I need a big kitchen. One bathroom is OK. There is no balcony in my flat now, but I'd like my new flat to have one.
（W: 我想要一個有三間臥室的大房子。我現在住在兩房的房子。但是我母親要來跟我們一起住。我需要一個大廚房。一間浴室是可以的。現在我的房子沒有陽台，但是我希望我的新房子有一個陽台。）

M: Do you want to live on Green Island?
（M: 你想住在 Green 島嗎？）

W: No, not Green Island. Do you have flats in Deepwater Bay?
（W: 不，不要 Green 島。你們在 Deepwater 海灣有房子嗎？）

M: Yes, there's a lovely flat near Deepwater Bay Road. It's 95 square metres. There are three bedrooms, a living room, a bathroom, a big kitchen and a balcony. It costs only 800,000 yuan.
（M: 有的，靠近 Deepwater Bay 路有一棟可愛的房子。它九十五平方公尺大。有三間臥室、一個客廳、一間浴室，一個大廚房和一個陽台。它只要八十萬元。）

W: That sounds nice. OK, I'll come later this afternoon to your office. Thank you very much. Goodbye.
（W: 那個聽起來很不錯。好。我今天晚一點會再來你的辦公室。非常感謝你。再見。）

	Mrs Wang's old flat	**The new flat she will buy**
place（地點）	In the city centre __25__ but noisy（在市中心____但很吵）	In the suburbs __26__（在郊區____）
bedroom（房間）	2	__27__
kitchen（廚房）	Small（小的）	__28__
balcony（陽台）	0	1
Size（大小）	／	__29__ m² （____平方公尺）
Cost（價格）	／	__30__ yuan（____元）

25. 答案：convenient (方便的)

26. 答案：quiet (安靜的)

27. 答案：3/three (三)

28. 答案：big (大的)

29. 答案：95/ninety-five (九十五)

30. 答案：800,000/eight hundred thousand (八十萬)

I、Listen and choose the right picture.（根據你聽到的內容,選出相應的圖片。）（6分）

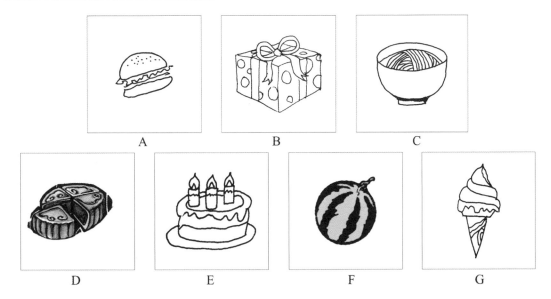

A   B   C

D   E   F   G

1. My brother's favourite food is ice cream.（我兄弟最喜歡的食物是冰淇淋。）
    答案：(G)

2. Christmas is always what children can't wait as they can receive presents.
    （孩子們總是等不及聖誕節因為他們可以收到禮物。）
    答案：(B)

3. Mid-autumn is coming and it's time to taste moon cakes.
    （中秋節要到了，是品嚐月餅的時候了。）
    答案：(D)

4. Eating noodles on birthday stands for a longer and healthier life.
    （在生日那天吃麵象徵著更長和更健康的人生。）
    答案：(C)

5. My favorite fast food restaurant is Burger King. I can find the best
    hamburgers there.（我最喜歡的速食餐廳是漢堡堡王。我可以在那裡找到最好的
    漢堡。）
    答案：(A)

6. We can also eat water melons in winter but at a higher price.
    （我們也可以在冬天吃到西瓜但是價錢比較貴。）

答案：(F)

7. M: What would you like for breakfast?（男：妳早餐想吃什麼？）

W: I want some eggs and bread. A cup of milk will be nice too.
（女：我想要一些蛋和麵包。一杯牛奶也會很好。）

M: Would you like some bacon?（男：妳想要一些培根嗎？）

W: No, thanks.（女：不，謝了。）

Q: What doesn't the woman want for breakfast?
（問題：這位女士早餐不想吃什麼？）

(A)Milk.（牛奶）　(B)Eggs.（蛋）　(C)Bacon.（培根）　(D)Bread.（麵包）

答案：(C)

8. M: When is your mother's birthday?（男：妳母親的生日是哪時候？）

W: It was yesterday, November 3rd.（女：是昨天，十一月三日。）

M: Really? I should have prepared a gift.（男：真的嗎？我應該準備個禮物的。）

Q: What's the date today?（問題：今天的日期是？）

(A)Nov. 2nd.（十一月二日）　　(B)Oct. 31st.（十月三十一日）

(C)Nov. 3rd.（十一月三日）　　(D)Nov. 4th.（十一月四日

答案：(D)

9. M: I will go to Hong Kong to spend my holiday.（男：我將去香港度假。）

W: That's cool. Will you go alone or with someone else?
（女：那真酷。你會獨自去還是和別人一起去？）

M: One of my colleagues will go with me as it is organized by my company.
（男：我的一位同事將和我一起去因為這是我的公司安排的。）

Q: Who will go with the man?（問題：誰將會和這位男士一起去？）

(A)His workmate.（他的工作夥伴。）　(B)His classmate.（他的同班同學。）

(C)His deskmate.（他的同桌夥伴。）　(D)His roommate.（他的室友。）

答案：(A)

10. M: Hurry up. Mom is waiting for us at the gate.（男：快點。媽媽在大門口等我們。）

W: But I have to hand in the assignment to Mrs. Wang. She wants to check it face to face.（女：但是我必須把這個作業繳交給王太太。她想要當面檢查它。）

M: Anyway. Be quick.（男：無論如何。快點。）

Q: Where does this dialogue take place?（問題：這段對話在哪裡發生？）

(A)At the cinema.（在電影院。）   (B)In the hospital.（在醫院。）

(C)At a library.（在圖書館。）   (D)At school.（在學校。）

答案：(D)

11. M: Can we meet at 3 in the afternoon?（男：我們可以在下午三點碰面嗎？）

    W: I think 3:30 may be fine as I have to give a report to my boss.

    （女：我想三點半好了，因為我必須交一份報告給我老闆。）

    M: OK. And I give you 30 more minutes. That will be enough for you to give a wonderful report.

    （男：好。我多給你三十分鐘。那將會足夠讓你交一份很讚的報告。）

    W: You are so nice. See you soon.（女：你人真好。待會見。）

    Q: When will they meet?（問題：他們將幾點碰面？）

(A)At 4 o'clock.（四點）   (B)At 3:30.（三點半）

(C)At 3 o'clock.（三點）   (D)At 2:30.（兩點半）

答案：(A)

12. M: Have you read the book I gave you yesterday?

    （男：妳讀了我昨天給妳的那本書嗎？）

    W: Yes. I always listen to you.（女：是啊。我總是聽你的話。）

    M: How do you like it?（男：你認為它如何？）

    W: To be frank, it is the last book that I want to read.

    （女：坦白說，那是我最不想讀的一本書。）

    Q: What does the girl think of the book?（問題：這位女孩認為這本書如何？）

(A)Exciting.（精彩）   (B)Meaningful.（有意義）

(C)Terrible.（糟糕）   (D)Interesting.（有趣）

答案：(C)

13. M: Who is the lady over there?（男：在那邊的那位女士是誰？）

    W: She is my aunt, a famous doctor in our town.

    （女：她是我阿姨，我們鎮上一位著名的醫師。）

    M: Then I know why I feel so familiar. Is her husband a policeman?

    （男：那我知道為什麼我看她那麼面熟了。她的丈夫是位警察嗎？）

    W: Yes. How do you know that?（女：對。你怎麼知道的？）

    M: He works with my father.（男：他和我父親一起工作。）

    Q: What is the boy's father's job?（問題：這位男孩的父親的工作是？）

(A)A doctor.（一位醫師。）   (B)A policeman.（一位警察。）

(C)A teacher.（一位教師。）   (D)A worker.（一位工人。）

答案：(B)

14. M: Would you mind my smoking here?（男：妳介意我在這裡抽菸嗎？）

W: I'm afraid you can't smoke here as my kid has had a sore throat.
（女：我恐怕妳不能在這裡抽菸因為我的小孩喉嚨痛。）

M: I'm so sorry and I will listen to you.（男：真抱歉，我會聽妳的話。）

Q: What happened to the lady's child?（問題：這位淑女的孩子怎麼了？）

(A)He smoked a lot.（他抽很多煙。）

(B)He began to smoke.（他開始抽菸。）

(C)He had a sore throat.（他喉嚨痛。）

(D)He threw the cigarettes away.（他把香菸丟掉。）

答案：(C)

15. M: I have ordered fried chicken and the rice with daily soup. What else do you want?（男：我點了炸雞和米飯配例湯。妳還想要什麼別的？）

W: Let me see. Oh, the pictures in the menu always make me confused.
（女：我看看。噢，菜單上的圖片總是讓我很迷惑。）

Q: Where are they now?（問題：他們現在在哪裡？）

(A)In a restaurant.（在一間餐廳裡。）　(B)At school.（在學校。）

(C)In the kitchen.（在廚房裡。）　(D)In a flower market.（在花卉市場。）

答案：(A)

16. M: Mrs. Lee, what have you learnt this term?
（男：李太太，妳這學期學到了什麼？）

W: I have learnt how to operate computers and how the piano is played.
（女：我學到了如何操作電腦和鋼琴是怎麼彈的。）

M: What else have you learnt?（男：另外妳還學到什麼？）

W: I have learnt taking good pictures this year and please support me.
（女：我今年學到如何拍好的照片，請支持我。）

M: Of course! But we wonder how you can do that.
（男：當然！但是我們不知道妳如何可以做到。）

W: Please remember, never too old to learn.（女：請記住，學習永遠不嫌老。）

Q: What can we learn from the woman's words?
（問題：從這位女士的話語中我們可以得知？）

(A)She is too old and she wants to give up learning more.
（她太老了她想放棄學更多。）

(B)She thinks it is wise to learn at one's early age.
（她認為在一個人年輕時學習是明智的。）

(C)She won't stop learning till her death.（她一直到死都不會停止學習。）

(D)She is afraid of learning too much as it wastes time.
（她害怕學習太多因為這會浪費時間。）

答案：(C)

Jim, who was twenty-one years old, got a job in a big factory in another town. He left home and found a comfortable flat. He lived there on his own.

吉姆，二十一歲，在另一個城鎮的大工廠裡得到一個工作。他離開家找到一間舒適的公寓。他獨自住在那裏。

At first he cleaned it himself, but he did not want to tire himself out, so he decided to find someone to do the housework. He asked a lot of his fellow workers at the factory what they did about this, and one of the men said, "Oh, Mrs. Roper cleans my flat. She washes the dishes, irons my shirts, keeps the place neat and tidy and so on. I'll introduce her to you if you like. She's a charming old lady." So the next evening Mrs. Roper came to see Jim, and she agreed with pleasure to come to his flat every morning and work for an hour.

起初他自己打掃，但他不想讓自己累壞，所以他決定找個人來做家事。他問了很多他在工廠的工作夥伴他們都怎麼處理，其中一位男士說，「喔，羅培太太打掃我的公寓。她洗碗盤，熨燙我的襯衫，維持環境整潔和之類的。如果你有興趣我會把她介紹給你。她是一位迷人的老婦人。」所以次日的晚上羅培太太來看吉姆，她欣然答應每天早上到他的公寓工作一小時。

After she worked for Jim for two weeks, he looked at the mirror in his bedroom and thought, "That mirror looks very dusty. Mrs. Roper must have forgotten to clean it." He wrote a message in the dust with his finger, "I'm coughing whenever I breathe because the mirror in this room is very dusty."

她為吉姆工作了兩星期之後，他看著他臥室的鏡子想到，「那面鏡子看起來很多灰塵。羅培太太一定是忘記擦它了。」他用他的手指在灰塵上留言道，「每當我呼吸我都咳嗽，因為這房間裡的鏡子有很多灰塵。」

He came home at seven o'clock that evening. Having eaten his supper, he went into his bedroom and looked at the mirror. "That silly woman still hasn't cleaned it!" he said to himself. "All it needs is a cloth!"

他那天晚上七點中回到家。吃了他的晚餐，他去他的臥室且看著那面鏡子。「那位笨女人仍然沒有擦它！」他對他自己說。「它所需要的只是一塊布！」

But then he bent down and in front of the mirror he saw a bottle which he had never seen. He picked it up and found some words on it. He read the words, "Cough medicine".

但是當他在鏡子前彎下腰來他看到一個從未見過的瓶子。他把它拿起來發現上面有些字。他讀了這些字，「咳嗽藥。」

17. Jim lived alone in another town as he worked there.
（吉姆在另一個城鎮獨自居住因為他在那邊工作。）
答案：(T 對)

18. Jim didn't like housework and he always made his flat dusty and untidy.
（吉姆不喜歡做家事，他總是把他的公寓弄得都是灰塵且很亂。）
答案：(F 錯)

19. Mrs. Roper was introduced to Jim and came to see Jim the next morning.
（羅培太太被介紹給吉姆，且在第二天早上來看吉姆。）
答案：(F 錯)

20. Jim left a message on a paper to tell Mrs. Roper to clean the mirror.
（吉姆在一張紙上留言叫羅培太太擦那面鏡子。）
答案：(F 錯)

21. Jim was always coughing badly whenever he breathed.
（每當吉姆呼吸，他總是咳嗽得很厲害。）
答案：(F 錯)

22. The cough medicine Mrs. Roper prepared would make Jim deeply moved.
（羅培太太所準備的咳嗽藥會讓吉姆深深感動。）
答案：(F 錯)

23. Mrs. Roper misunderstood Jim's message.（羅培太太誤會了吉姆的留言。）
答案：(T 對)

IV、Listen to the passage and fill in the blanks with proper words.（聽短文,用最恰當的詞填空,每格限填一詞）（共 7 分）

Having healthy skin tells others that you take good care of yourself. This is very attractive to every type of person. Like the heart and the stomach, skin is a part of your body. It protects you and keeps you from getting sick. How to take care of your skin? — Read on for some tips.

有健康的皮膚就是告訴其他人你把自己照顧得很好。這對每一種人都很有吸引力。像心臟和胃，皮膚是你身體的一部分。它保護你且讓你不會生病。如何照顧你的皮膚？——繼續往下讀一些技巧。

One simple way is to keep your skin clean. Keeping your hands clean is very important because your hands can spread germs to somewhere in your body.

一個簡單的方法是維持你的皮膚清潔。維持你的手乾淨是很重要的，因為你的手可以將細菌散布到你身體的某處。

When washing your hands, you can use warm water and mild soap. You should wash everywhere carefully, such as the palms, the parts between the fingers, and under the nails.

當你洗手時，你可以用溫水和溫和的肥皂。你應仔細地清洗每個地方，像是手心，手指之間，和指甲下面。

When you take a bath, you should use warm water to clean your body. Don't forget to clean the parts under your arms or behind your ears! Pay attention to your face, especially when you are young. It's a good idea to wash your face once or twice daily with warm water.

當你泡澡，你應用溫水清潔你的身體。別忘了清潔你腋下的部分或耳朵背後！留意你的臉，特別是當你年輕的時候。每天用溫水洗臉一兩次是個好主意。

Besides, drink enough water. Water can make your skin softer and brighter.

另外，喝足夠的水。水可以讓你的皮膚更柔軟且更明亮。

Taking good care of your skin today will keep you away from future problems.

今天好好照顧你的皮膚將讓你遠離未來的問題。

- Healthy skin is __24__ to all kinds of people.
  （健康的肌膚對每一種人都很有吸引力。）
- Keeping your hands clean can stop germs from being __25__ to other places.（維持你的手清潔可以阻止細菌散布到其他地方。）
- We'd better use warm water and mild __26__ to wash hands.
  （我們最好用溫水和溫和的肥皂洗手。）
- Remember to clean the __27__ under your arms or behind your ears during a bath.
  （在泡澡時記得要清潔你腋下的部分或你耳朵背後。）
- It is wise to wash your face once or twice __28__ with warm water.
  （每天用溫水洗一兩次臉是明智的。）
- Drinking enough water makes your skin brighter and __29__.
  （喝足夠的水讓你的皮膚更明亮且更柔軟。）
- You will have fewer __30__ problems if you take good care of your skin.
  （你會有較少未來的問題如果你好好照顧你的皮膚。）

24. 答案：attractive（吸引力）
25. 答案：spread（散布）
26. 答案：soap（肥皂）
27. 答案：parts（部分）
28. 答案：daily（每日）
29. 答案：softer（更柔軟）
30. 答案：future（未來）

全新國中會考英語聽力精選(中)原文及參考答案

Unit 8

I、Listen and choose the right picture.（根據你所聽到的內容,選出相應的圖片。）（6分）

1. You mustn't throw rubbish on the ground.（你不可以把垃圾丟在地上。）

答案：(G)

2. Peter's father works in a restaurant. He is a cook.
   （Peter 的父親在餐廳工作。他是一位廚師。）

答案：(A)

3. The sign on the wall says "No smoking".（牆上的標示寫著：「禁止吸菸」。）

答案：(F)

4. Little Kitty often helps her teacher carry books to the teachers' office.
   （小 Kitty 常常幫她的老師把書拿去教師辦公室。）

答案：(B)

5. I have a new net-pal who is an American.（我有一個新網友，是美國人。）

答案：(D)

6. My sister is good at playing the flute.（我姊姊擅長吹長笛。）

答案：(C)

7. What can I do for you, sir?（先生，我能為你效勞嗎？）
   (A)Yes, I do.（是的，我做。）
   (B)All right.（好。）
   (C)I'd like a cup of coffee.（我想要一杯咖啡。）
   (D)No, you needn't.（不，你不需要。）
   答案：(C)

8. How do you go to school every day?（你每天怎麼去學校？）
   (A)By foot.（用腳。）
   (B)On foot.（步行。）
   (C)By my father's car.（搭我爸的車。）
   (D)On car.（在公車。）
   答案：(B)

9. Nice to meet you, Kitty.（Kitty 很高興認識你。）
   (A)You too.（你也是。）
   (B)Thank you.（謝謝你。）
   (C)Nice to meet you, too.（也很高興認識你。）
   (D)Hello.（哈囉。）
   答案：(C)

10. You've done a wonderful job.（你做得太棒了。）
    (A)Thanks.（謝謝。）   (B)No, it isn't.（不，它不是。）
    (C)Yes, I do.（是，我是。）   (D)No problem.（沒問題。）
    答案：(A)

11. Which is more important, math or Chinese?（數學和中文那一個比較重要？）
    (A)Each.（每一個。）   (B)No, they aren't.（不，他們不重要。）
    (C)It's hard to say.（這很難說。）   (D)Yes, they are.（是的，它們是。）
    答案：(C)

12. My grandfather has got a bad cold.（我祖父感冒很嚴重。）
    (A)He will be good.（他會是好的。）
    (B)It's OK.（那還好。）
    (C)I'm sorry to hear that.（我很抱歉聽到這件事。）
    (D)That's great!（太棒了！）
    答案：(C)

13. W: Which city do you like best?（W: 你最喜歡哪一個城市？）

    M: I lived in Beijing when I was young. Now I live in Shanghai, but my favourite city is Hangzhou, so I hope to move there in the future.

    （M: 年輕的時候我住在北京。我現在住在上海,但是我最喜歡的城市是杭州。所以我希望將來搬去那兒。）

    Q: Which city does the man live in?（Q: 這個男人住在哪個城市？）

    (A)Hangzhou.（杭州。）　　　　　　(B)Shanghai.（上海。）

    (C)Beijing.（北京。）　　　　　　　(D)Guangzhou.（廣州。）

    答案：(B)

14. W: I can't find my suitcase.（W: 我找不到我的行李箱。）

    M: You can go to the Lost and Found office. Maybe somebody found it.

    （M: 你可以去失物招領處。或許有人發現它。）

    W: OK. Where is it?（W: 好。在哪裡？）

    M: Just over there, next to the bank.（M: 就在那兒,銀行的隔壁。）

    Q: Where does the dialogue probably happen?（Q: 這段對話大概在哪裡發生？）

    (A)In a bank.（在銀行。）　　　　　(B)At a restaurant.（在餐廳。）

    (C)In an office.（在辦公室。）　　　(D)At the airport.（在機場。）

    答案：(D)

15. W: The mooncakes with nuts in them are very delicious. Please have a taste of them.(W: 有堅果的月餅非常好吃。請嚐嚐看。）

    M: Oh, no, thanks. I can't have any more.（M: 不用了,謝謝。我再也吃不下了。）

    Q: Why doesn't the man want to eat the mooncakes?

    （Q: 這個男人為什麼不想吃月餅？）

    (A)They are not delicious.（它們不好吃。）

    (B)He is hungry.（他餓了。）

    (C)He is full.（他飽了。）

    (D)He doesn't like mooncakes.（他不喜歡月餅。）

    答案：(C)

16. W: What day is it today?（W: 今天星期幾？）

    M: It's Wednesday. When are we going to visit Jinmao Building?

    （M: 今天星期三。我們甚麼時候去參觀金茂大樓？）

    W: Oh, we're going to visit it the day after tomorrow.（W: 喔,我們後天去參觀。）

    M: I think we'll have a good time there.（M: 我想我們在那裡會很開心。）

    Q: When are they going to visit Jinmao Building?

（Q: 他們甚麼時候去參觀金茂大樓？）
(A)Two days later.（兩天後。）　　　　(B)Tomorrow.（明天。）
(C)Wednesday.（星期三。）　　　　　(D)Monday.（星期一。）
答案：(A)

17. W: Hello, Tom. You look tired today.（W: 哈囉，Tom。你今天看起來很累。）

　　M: Yes. I went to bed too late last night.（M: 是的。我昨天晚上太晚睡了。）

　　W: You'd better go to bed earlier this evening.（W: 你今天晚上最好早點睡。）

　　M: But tomorrow we will have an exam. I'll do some revision.
　　　　（M: 但是明天我們有一場考試。我要復習。）

　　W: If you don't have enough rest, you won't do well in the exam.
　　　　（W: 如果你休息得不夠，你會考不好的。）

　　Q: What is the girl's suggestion to Tom?（Q: 女孩給了 Tom 甚麼建議？）
　　(A)Do some revision.（復習。）　　　(B)Have a good rest.（好好休息。）
　　(C)Go to bed late.（晚點睡。）　　　(D)Do well in English.（讀好英文。）
　　答案：(B)

18. W: I was born in 1982. What about you?（W: 我一九八二年生。你呢？）

　　M: I was born in 1983. My sister is two years younger than me.
　　　　（M: 我一九八三年生。我妹妹比我小兩歲。）

　　W: Do you go to the same school?（W: 你們去同樣的學校嗎？）

　　M: Yes. But we are not in the same class.（M: 是的。但是我們在不同班級。）

　　Q: The girl is younger than the boy, isn't she?（Q: 女孩比男孩年輕，是嗎？）
　　(A)No, she isn't.（不，她不是。）　　　(B)No, she is.（不，她是。）
　　(C)Yes, she is.（是，她是。）　　　　(D)Yes, she isn't.（是，她不是。）
　　答案：(A)

IV、Listen to the dialogue and decide whether the following statements are True (T) or False (F).（判斷下列句子內容是否符合你所聽到的對話內容,符合的用"T"表示,不符合的用"F"表示。）（6分）

　　New Zealand is a country in Australia. It lies in the south part of the world. There is an old story in New Zealand. It says that the God separated his parents, the Sky and the Earth, to create the world we live in. This story was brought to the World Expo 2010 by the New Zealand Pavilion under the theme "Cities of Nature: Living between Land and Sky". The pavilion has an area of 2,000 square metres. It has three parts: the welcoming space, the interior, and the roof garden.

　　紐西蘭是在澳洲大陸的一個國家。它位於南半球。紐西蘭有一個古老的故事。故事描述上帝隔離了祂的父母，天空與陸地，來創造我們所居住的世界。這個故事是由紐西蘭展示館，在「自然城市：生活在陸地與天空之間」的主題下，向二零一零年世界博覽會所提出的。這個展示館佔地兩千平方公尺。它分為三個部分：歡迎區、內展區，以及屋頂花園。

The welcoming space was in front of the pavilion. There were many young people who could speak Chinese well in the welcoming space at the Expo. They introduced the culture and history of New Zealand to the visitors. When people entered the pavilion, they could experience a day in a New Zealand city starting from the sea, through the suburbs, the city centre and the mountains.

歡迎區在展示館的前方。世博會的歡迎區有非常多會說中文的年輕人。他們向參觀者介紹紐西蘭的文化和歷史。當人們進入展示館時，他們可以從海洋開始、到郊區、市中心與山區，來體驗紐西蘭城市的一天 。

19. New Zealand is in South America. （紐西蘭在南美洲。）
    答案：(F 錯)

20. The old story in New Zealand says the God's parents created the world we live in.
    （紐西蘭的古老故事描述了上帝的父母創造了我們所居住的世界。）
    答案：(F 錯)

21. The theme of the New Zealand Pavilion is "Better city, better life".
    （紐西蘭展示館的主題是「更好的城市、更好的生活」。）
    答案：(F 錯)

22. The pavilion has an area of 2,000 square meters. （展示館佔地兩千平方公尺。）
    答案：(T 對)

23. There are four parts in the New Zealand Pavilion. （紐西蘭展示館有四個部分。）
    答案：(F 錯)

24. When people entered the pavilion, they could experience a day in a New Zealand city.
    （當人們進入展示館時，他們可以體驗紐西蘭城市的一天。）
    答案：(T 對)

V、Listen and fill in the blanks.（根據你所聽到的內容,用適當的單詞完成下面的句子。每空格限填一詞。）（6分）

Many people ask me the question: When is the best time to visit Shanghai? Usually, I couldn't give an answer. However, these days, when I walk on Nanjing Road or visit the Bund at night, I regret that I didn't tell my friends that September may be the best time to visit Shanghai. Why? Because the Shanghai Travel Festival starts in September every year.

許多人問我這個問題：甚麼時候遊覽上海是最好的時間？通常我不給答案。但是，當我這幾天晚上去南京路或外灘走走的時候，我很後悔我沒告我的朋友，九月可能是遊覽上海最好的時間。為什麼呢？因為上海旅遊節每年九月展開。

There are many activities during the festival. It lasts for about three weeks. There are carnivals, boat shows on the Huangpu River, International Firework Show, F1 Race, Beer Festival, Germany Week and so on. There are also many other international events during the three weeks in Shanghai.

在旅遊節的期間有非常多活動。歷時約三個星期。有嘉年華會、黃浦江上的船隻表演、國際煙火秀，FI 賽車，啤酒節，德國週…等等。在那個三星期裡，上海也有許多其他國際性的活動。

During the Travel Festival, all the lights will be turned on. The whole city is so beautiful. I believe that 50％ of the beauty of Shanghai is its lights.

在旅遊節期間，所有的燈光都點亮了。整個城市是如此的美麗。我相信上海百分之五十的美就是來自它的燈光。

Also, it is cooling down and sunny. The weather is great. The lights are great. September should be the best time to visit Shanghai!

還有，天氣涼爽而且晴朗。天氣很棒。燈光很棒。九月應該就是遊覽上海最好的時間！

25. Usually, I couldn't give an <u>answer</u> when people ask me the question: when is the best time to visit Shanghai?

當有人問我這個問題：甚麼時候是遊覽上海最好的時間？我通常不給<u>答案</u>。

26. <u>September</u> may be the best time to visit Shanghai.

<u>九月</u>或許就是遊覽上海最好的時間。

27. There are many <u>activities</u> during the Shanghai Travel <u>festival</u>.

在上海旅遊<u>節</u>的期間有非常多<u>活動</u>。

28. There are also many other <u>international</u> events during the three weeks in Shanghai.

在那三個星期中，上海也有許多其他<u>國際性</u>的活動。

29. I believe that <u>50%</u> of the beauty of Shanghai is its lights.

我相信上海百分之<u>百分之五十</u>的美就是來自它的燈光。

Unit 9

Ⅰ、Listen and choose the right picture.（根據你所聽到的內容，選出相應的圖片。）（6分）

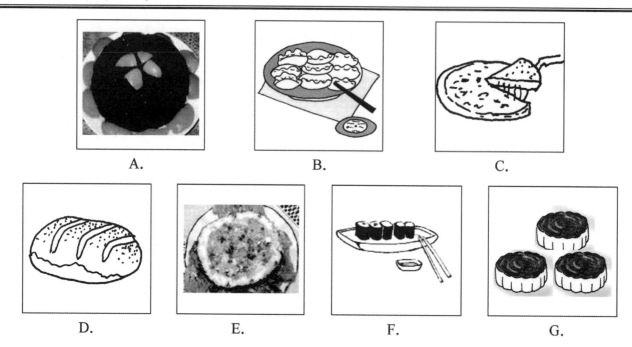

A.　　　　　　　　B.　　　　　　　　C.

D.　　　　　　　　E.　　　　　　　　F.　　　　　　　　G.

1.　I want to go to a Japanese restaurant tonight. I like eating sushi.
　　（我今晚想去日本餐廳。我喜歡吃壽司。）
　　答案：(F)

2.　Shanghainese usually have some Chinese rice pudding at the end of the special dinner on Chinese New Year's Eve.
　　（上海人通常在除夕夜的特殊晚餐之後吃一些中國米布丁(八寶飯)。）
　　答案：(A)

3.　Why not have some dumplings? They are really delicious.
　　（為什麼不吃餃子呢？他們非常好吃。）
　　答案：(B)

4.　Americans usually have hot dogs for lunch. They usually have a quick lunch.
　　（美國人通常午餐吃熱狗。他們通常吃快速(簡易)午餐。）
　　答案：(D)

5.　Pizzahut was a very small fast-food shop which sold only pizzas. But now it has already become a chain store all over the world.

（Pizzahut 以前是一間只賣披薩的小型速食店。但是現在已經是一間全世界的連鎖店了。）

答案：(C)

6. Did you taste the tasty pineapple fried rice when you were on holiday in Thailand?
（你在泰國度假的時候，你吃了好吃可口的鳳梨炒飯嗎？）

答案：(E)

II、Listen and choose the best response to the sentence you hear.（根據你所聽到的句子，選出最恰當的應答句。）（6分）

7. Let's have an international food festival. We can sell foods from different countries in the world.
（我們來辦個國際美食節吧。我們可以賣世界上不同國家的食物。）

(A)What is an international food festival?（國際美食節是甚麼？）

(B)Let's go to school to attend the food festival.（我們去學校參加美食節吧。）

(C)Yes. It'll be great fun.（好。那一定很有趣。）

(D)Thank you very much.（非常感謝你。）

答案：(C)

8. I like Chinese food best.
（我最喜歡中國食物。）

(A)I will sell fish and chips and raisin scones.（我要賣炸魚薯條和葡萄烤餅(司康)）

(B)I will sell pineapple fried rice and prawn cakes.（我要賣鳳梨炒飯和蝦餅。）

(C)I will sell hot dogs and apple pies.（我要賣熱狗和蘋果派。）

(D)I will sell rice dumplings and moon cakes.（我要賣湯圓和月餅。）

答案：(D)

9. Can you show me how to make raisin scones, please?
（請你告訴我怎麼做葡萄烤餅(司康)好嗎？）

(A)Thank you.（謝謝你。）

(B)Of course.（當然。）

(C)My pleasure.（我的榮幸。）

(D)That's all right.（沒關係。）

答案：(B)

10. May I have two raisin scones and a plate of fish and chips, please?
（請給我兩個葡萄烤餅(司康)和一盤炸魚薯條好嗎？）

(A)Yes, please.（是的，請。）

(B)Yes, thank you.（好的，謝謝你。）

(C)Yes, very good.（是的，非常好。）

(D)Yes, of course.（好的，當然。）

答案：(D)

11. How much are they in all?

（他們一共多少錢？）

(A)Fifty yuan altogether.（一共五十元。）

(B)There are ten.（有十個。）

(C)It's ten yuan.（那個是十元。）

(D)Five kilograms.（五公斤。）

答案：(A)

12. How are you and Ben?

（你和 Ben 好嗎？）

(A)How are you?（你好嗎？）

(B)We are in the USA now.（我們現在在美國。）

(C)Fine. And you?（很好。你呢？）

(D)Are you sure?（你確定嗎？）

答案：(C)

Ⅲ、Listen to the dialogue and choose the best answer to the question you hear.（根據你所聽到的對話和問題，選出最恰當的答案。）（6分）

13. W: Hi, Tom. Which would you like, a cup of tea or a glass of milk?

（W: 嗨，Tom。你想要一杯茶或一杯牛奶？）

M: Do you mind if I just have a glass of water?
（M: 如果我只要一杯水，你介意嗎？）

W: Not at all.
（W: 一點也不介意。）

Question: What would Tom like to drink?
（問題：Tom 想喝甚麼？）

(A)A glass of milk.（一杯牛奶。）

(B)A glass of water.（一杯水。）

(C)A cup of tea.（一杯茶。）

(D)Nothing.（什麼都不喝。）

答案：(B)

14. W: Yesterday I went to see a film called Hero. What about you?
（W: 昨天我去看了場電影叫做 Hero。你呢？）

M: I watched a football match instead of seeing a film.
（M: 我沒去看電影但是去看了足球賽。）

Question: What did the man do yesterday?
（問題：男人昨天做了甚麼？）

(A)She went to the cinema.（她去看電影。）

(B)He watched TV at home.（他在家看電視。）

(C)He watched a football match.（他看足球賽。）

(D)He saw a film and watched a football match.（他看電影和足球賽。）

答案：(C)

15. W: Bob, is your school far from your home?
（W: Bob，你家離學校很遠嗎？）

M: Not so far, Mary. So I go to school on foot every day.
（M: Mary，不太遠。所以我每天走路上學。）

W: But I have to go to school by bus.
（W: 可是我要搭公車上學。）

Question: How does Bob go to school?
（問題：Bob 如何去學校？）

(A)By bike.（騎腳踏車。）

(B)On foot.（走路。）

(C)By bus.（搭公車。）

(D)By underground.（搭地鐵。）

答案：(B)

16. W: What's wrong with you?
（W: 你怎麼了？）

M: I have a headache.
（M: 我頭痛。）

W: You have had a cold. Take this medicine, and you'll be all right soon.
（W: 你感冒了。吃這個藥你很快就會好了。）

Question: Where are they?
（問題：他們在哪裡？）

(A)At the post office.（郵局。）

(B)In the hospital. （醫院。）

(C)At the supermarket. （超級市場。）

(D)In the classroom. （教室。）

答案：(B)

17. W: What are you going to do this weekend, Danny?
   （W: Danny，這個周末你要做甚麼？）

   M: I'm going to visit my aunt.
   （M: 我要去拜訪我姑姑。）

   W: Your aunt? Isn't she living in the city?
   （W: 你姑姑？他不住在這個城市嗎？）

   M: She used to live in the city. But now she's living in a village in a small
   town. She likes the quiet place.
   （M: 她以前住在市裡。但是她搬到一個小鎮的農村裡了。她喜歡安靜的地
   方。）

   Question: Where does Danny's aunt live?
   （問題：Danny 的姑姑住在哪裡？）

   (A)In the city. （城市。）

   (B)In the village. （農村。）

   (C)In a small town. （一個小鎮。）

   (D)In a quiet flat. （安靜的房子。）

   答案：(B)

18. M: We will have more computer lessons next year.
   （M: 我們明年會有更多電腦課。）

   W: I hope we could have more cookery lessons instead.
   （W: 我反而希望我們可以有更多烹飪課。）

   Question: What subject does the woman prefer?
   （問題：那個女人比較喜歡甚麼科目？）

   (A)Cookery lessons. （烹飪課。）

   (B)Computer lessons. （電腦課。）

   (C)Neither. （都不喜歡。）

   (D)Both. （都喜歡。）

   答案：(A)

IV、Listen to the passage and decide whether the following statements are True (T) or False (F). (判斷下列句子內容是否符合你所聽到的短文內容，符合的用"T"表示，不符合的用"F"表示。)（6分）

Most people make their living with their hands.
（大部分的人以手維生。）

But Tom makes his living with his feet.
（但是 Tom 以他的腳維生。）

A very good living it is, too.
（也是非常好的生活。）

Tom's story begins in a very small city in England.
（Tom 的故事起緣於一個英國的小城市。）

His parents are very poor.
（他的父母非常貧窮。）

Seven people live in their small house.
（七個人住在他們的小屋子裡。）

Tom has no place to play but in the street.
（除了街上以外，Tom 沒有地方可以玩耍。）

Tom's father often plays football.
（Tom 的父親偶爾踢足球。）

Little Tom wants to play football, too.
（小 Tom 也想踢足球。）

So his father makes a soft ball for him to kick.
（所以他的父親做了一個軟的球讓他踢。）

It is a sock filled with pieces of cloth.
（那是一個塞滿了布料的襪子。）

The little boy kicks it every day.
（小男孩每天踢它。）

At last Tom learns to kick a real football, and after a few years he can play football very well.
（最後，Tom 學習踢真的足球，而且在數年之後，他可以踢得非常好。）

Now Tom is one of the best football players in the world.
（現在，Tom 是世界上最好的足球員之一。）

19. Tom's parents have little money.
（Tom 父母的錢不多。）

答案：(T 對)

20. Tom's father can't buy a real football for him.

（Tom 的父親買不了真的足球給他。）

答案：（T 對）

21. Both Tom and his father like playing football.
（Tom 和他的父親都喜歡踢足球。）

答案：（T 對）

22. Tom is the best football player in the world.
（Tom 是世界上最好的足球員。）

答案：（F 錯）

23. Tom makes his living with his hands.
（Tom 以手維生。）

答案：（F 錯）

24. Tom's mother also likes playing football, too.
（Tom 的母親也喜歡踢足球。）

答案：（F 錯）

Ⅴ、Listen and fill in the blanks.（根據你所聽到的內容，用適當的單詞完成下面的句子。每空格限填一詞。）（6分）

In the year 2050, there will be different kinds of materials for clothes.
（在 2050 年，衣物將有各種不同的材質。）

Special chemicals will make the clothes keep clean — they will never get dirty, and they will never smell.
（特殊化學物質將使衣物保持乾淨——他們永遠不會變髒，也不會有異味。）

We will save water and money.
（我們將省水與省錢。）

We won't worry about what to wear to school every day.
（我們不再擔心每天要穿甚麼衣服上學。）

Children won't go to school.
（孩子們不必去學校。）

They will stay at home in front of their computers.
（他們將在他們家裡的電腦前。）

Children can wear their favorite Saturday clothes.
（孩子們可以穿他們最喜歡的周末服裝。）

It will be fun.
（那將會很有趣。）

What do you think?

（你認為怎麼樣呢？）

Do you think it will be fun?

（你覺得那會很有趣嗎？）

What do you think school clothes and school life will be like in 2050?

（你覺得 2050 年的校服和學校生活會是怎麼樣呢？）

In __25__, there will be different kinds of materials for clothes.

（在____年，衣物將有各種不同的材質。）

Clothes with special chemicals will never get __26__.

（有了特殊化學物質的衣物將永遠不會變____。）

People will save __27__ and money.

（人們將省下____和金錢。）

Students won't need to __28__ about what to wear to school every day.

（學生們不需要____每天穿甚麼衣服上學。）

Students will stay at home in front of their __29__.

（學生們將會在他們家裡的____前。）

What do you think of the future life? Do you think it will be __30__?

（你覺得未來生活會是怎樣呢？你覺得那會很____嗎？）

25. 答案：2050

26. 答案：dirty (骯髒的)

27. 答案：water (水)

28. 答案：worry (擔心)

29. 答案：computers (電腦)

30. 答案：fun (趣味)

Unit 10

I、**Listen and choose the right picture.**（根據你所聽到的內容,選出相應的圖片。）（6分）

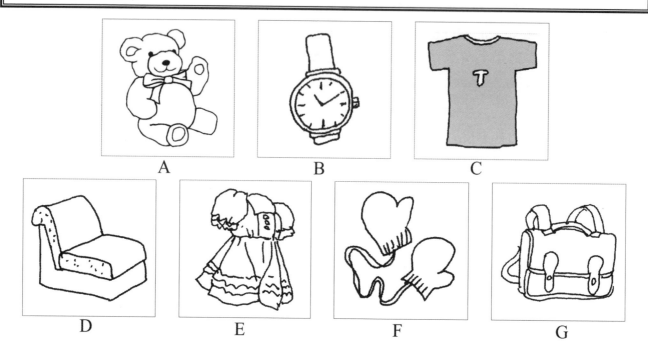

1. My little brother's birthday is coming. I'm going to buy him a toy bear.
   （我弟弟的生日快到了。我要買一個泰迪熊給他。）
   答案：(A)

2. Mr. Lin bought a new sofa for his new flat.
   （Lin 先生為他的新公寓買了一套新沙發。）
   答案：(D)

3. Peter has sent his daughter a new dress. （Peter 送了一件新洋裝給他的女兒。）
   答案：(E)

4. It's convenient for us to wear T-shirts in summer.
   （夏天穿 T 恤對我們來說很方便。）
   答案：(C)

5. If you want to buy a school bag, you can go to the stationery store.
（如果你想買書包，你可以去文具店。）

答案：(G)

6. You can buy a watch on the fourth floor.（你可以到四樓買手錶。）

答案：(B)

II、Listen and choose the best response to the sentence you hear.（根據你所聽到的句子,選出最恰當的應答句。）（6分）

---

7. What size do you wear?（你穿幾號？）
    (A)Shirts.（襯衫。）   (B)Sports shoes.（運動鞋。）
    (C)Size medium.（中號。）   (D)Clothes.（服裝。）

答案：(C)

8. Can I have a look at that pair of jeans?（我可以看看那條牛仔褲嗎？）
    (A)No, you can't.（不，你不可以。）
    (B)The jeans are over there.（牛仔褲在那邊。）
    (C)Sure.（當然可以。）
    (D)I don't like the color.（我不喜歡這個顏色。）

答案：(C)

9. I'm terribly sorry to bother you.（很抱歉打擾到你 。）
    (A)It doesn't matter.（沒關係。）   (B)No, you don't.（不，你沒打擾。）
    (C)Yes, you do.（是的，你打擾了。）   (D)Don't bother me.（別打擾我。）

答案：(A)

10. We're going to have a ball. Would you like to join us?
    （我們要辦一個舞會。你想參加嗎？）
    (A)What's the matter?（怎麼了？）
    (B)Sure. What time?（當然。幾點？）
    (C)Yes, I do.（是的，我願意。）
    (D)The ball will be at my place.（舞會將會在我住的地方。）

答案：(B)

11. I prefer jeans with blue belts to the ones with yellow belts.
    （比起配上黃色腰帶的，我比較喜歡配上藍色腰帶的牛仔褲。）
    (A)So do I.（我也是。）   (B)So I do.（我這麼做的。）
    (C)Neither do I.（我也不是。）   (D)Neither I do.（我也不這麼做。）

答案：(A)

12. What is the duration of that film?（那部電影歷時多久？）

(A)Three hours.（三小時。） (B)In three hours.（在三小時以內。）
(C)At three o'clock.（在三點。） (D)Since three hours.（自三小時開始。）
答案：(A)

Ⅲ、Listen to the dialogue and choose the best answer to the question you hear.（根據你所聽到的對話和問題,選出最恰當的答案。）（6分）

13. W: Can I help you?（W: 我能為你服務嗎？）
    M: Yes. I bought this pair of shoes here yesterday. I like the style, but can you change them for white ones? I don't like black ones.
    （M: 是的。我昨天在這裡買了這雙鞋。我喜歡這個樣式,但是你能換成白色的嗎？我不喜歡黑色的。）
    Q: Why does the man want to change the shoes?（Q: 那個男人為什麼想換鞋？）
    (A)He doesn't like the style.（他不喜歡那個樣式。）
    (B)He doesn't like the colour.（他不喜歡那個顏色。）
    (C)The size is too big.（尺寸太大。）
    (D)The size is too small.（尺寸太小。）
    答案：(B)

14. M: How much are the tomatoes?（M: 番茄多少錢？）
    W: They are four yuan a kilo.（W: 一公斤四元。）
    M: I'll take two kilos, please.（M: 請給我兩公斤。）
    Q: How much should the man pay for the tomatoes?
    （Q: 那個男人要花多少錢買番茄？）
    (A)4 yuan.（四元。） (B)8 yuan.（八元。）
    (C)12 yuan.（十二元。） (D)14 yuan.（十四元。）
    答案：(B)

15. M: Lucy, you look really cool in the glasses.（M: Lucy,妳戴眼鏡看起來好酷。）
    W: Thank you. I think Nancy also looks nice in that hat.
    （W: 謝謝你。我覺得 Nancy 戴那頂帽子也很好看。）
    M: So she does.（M: 沒錯。）
    Q: What does Lucy wear?（Q: Lucy 戴甚麼？）
    (A)A hat.（帽子。） (B)Bracelet.（手鐲。）
    (C)Earrings.（耳環。） (D)Glasses.（眼鏡。）
    答案：(D)

16. M: How long have you studied in this school?（M: 你在這所學校念了多久？）
    W: For three years. And I'll study for another three years.（W: 有三年了。我還要再念三年。）

Q: How long should the girl study in her school altogether?
（Q: 女孩在她的學校唸書一共要多久時間？）
(A)For three years.（三年。）   (B)For four years.（四年。）
(C)For five years.（五年。）   (D)For six years.（六年。）
答案：(D)

17. W: How nice your shoes are! How much did you pay for them?
   （W: 你的鞋子真好看。你花多少錢買的？）
   M: 15 dollars.（M: 十五元。）
   W: I like them very much. How much must I pay for a pair of women's shoes?
     （W: 我非常喜歡。我買一雙女鞋要花多少錢呢？）
   M: 5 dollars more.（M: 再多五元。）
   Q: How much is a pair of women's shoes?（Q: 女鞋一雙多少錢？）
   (A)10 dollars.（十元。）   (B)15 dollars.（十五元。）
   (C)20 dollars.（二十元。）   (D)25 dollars.（二十五元。）
   答案：(C)

18. W: Can I help you, sir?（W: 先生，我能為你服務嗎？）
   M: Yes. I need a sweater.（M: 是的。我需要一件毛衣。）
   W: What about this black one?（W: 這件黑色的怎麼樣？）
   M: Do you have it in size large?（M: 你有大號尺寸的嗎？）
   W: Of course.（W: 當然有。）
   Q: Where are they now?（Q: 他們現在在哪裡？）
   (A)At a clothes shop.（在服裝店。）   (B)In a restaurant.（在餐廳。）
   (C)At an office.（在辦公室。）   (D)In the fire station.（在消防局。）
   答案：(A)

IV、Listen to the dialogue and decide whether the following statements are True (T) or False (F).（判斷下列句子內容是否符合你所聽到的對話內容,符合的用"T"表示,不符合的用"F"表示。）（6分）

Lin Miaoke, a nine-year-old Beijing girl, has become one of the biggest stars after the 2008 Beijing Olympic Opening Ceremony. Lin Miaoke sang the song "A Hymn to My Motherland" at the opening ceremony of Beijing Olympic Games. Her sweet smile and beautiful voice touched almost everyone who was watching the opening ceremony.

林妙可，一名九歲大的北京女孩，在二零零八北京奧運開幕式之後變成了大明星。林妙可在北京奧運開幕式上唱了一首叫做「A Hymn to My Motherland(歌唱祖國)」的歌曲。她甜美的笑容與優美的嗓音幾乎感動了觀賞開幕式的每一個人。

The nine-year-old girl is now studying at West Street Primary School in Dongchun District, Beijing. Besides singing, she also likes folk dancing, playing the piano and flute.

She first came in a television advertisement with actress Zhao Wei at the age of six. In 2007, she appeared in a TV advertisement with Olympic champion Liu Xiang and an advertisement for the Beijing Olympics.

這名九歲大的女孩現在在北京東城區的西街小學念書。除了唱歌以外，她也喜歡跳土風舞、彈鋼琴和吹長笛。她六歲的時候第一次與女明星趙薇演出電視廣告。二零零七年，她與奧運冠軍劉翔在北京奧運的廣告上一起出現。

The famous director Zhang Yimou chose her among thousands of children in Beijing. Lin Miaoke is very famous now. Now we can see her pictures on many newspapers and magazines.

知名導演張藝謀從北京上千名兒童中挑選了她。林妙可現在非常有名。我們可以在許多報章雜誌上看到她的相片。

19. Lin Miaoke became famous after the 2008 Beijing Olympic Games.
   （林妙可在二零零八北京奧運之後成名。）
   答案：(T 對)

20. Lin Miaoke sang the song "A Hymn to My motherland" at the opening ceremony.
   （林妙可在開幕式上唱了一首歌叫做「A Hymn to My motherland」。）
   答案：(T 對)

21. She likes playing the piano and flute, but she can't dance.
   （她喜歡彈鋼琴和吹長笛，但是她不跳舞。）
   答案：(F 錯)

22. She was six years old when she appeared in the TV advertisement with Liu Xiang. （當她與劉翔一起出現在電視廣告上的時候，她六歲大。）
   答案：(F 錯)

23. The director Zhang Yimou chose her among all the children in Shanghai.
   （導演張藝謀從上海所有的兒童中挑選了她。）
   答案：(F 錯)

24. Now we can see her photos on many newspapers and magazines.
   （現在我們可以在許多報章雜誌上看到她的相片。）
   答案：(T 對)

V、Listen and fill in the blanks.（根據你所聽到的內容,用適當的單詞完成下面的句子。每空格限填一詞。）（6分）

M: Good morning. What can I do for you, lady?（M: 早安。小姐，我能為妳效勞嗎？）
W: I want to buy a pair of sports shoes of size 8.（W: 我想買一雙尺寸八號的鞋子。）
M: What about the black pair? It's 200 dollars.

（M: 那雙黑色的怎麼樣？那雙兩百元。）

W: It's smart but too expensive. Can you show me another pair?

（W: 很時髦但是太貴了。你能介紹其他雙鞋子嗎？）

M: The white pair is nice. Will you try them on?

（W: 這雙白色的不錯。你要不要試試看？）

W: Yes, they fit me very well. How much then?（W: 它非常適合我。要多少錢？）

M: 50 dollars cheaper.（M: 便宜五十元。）

W: All right. I'll take them. By the way, how much is the T-shirt with stripes?

（W: 好。我買了。另外，條紋 T 恤多少錢？）

M: The one with red stripes is 80 dollars, and the one with blue stripes is 40 dollars.（M: 紅色條紋的八十元，藍色條紋的四十元。）

W: I'll take the red one.（W: 我要紅色的。）

M: OK. So you want a pair of white sports shoes and a T-shirt with red stripes.

（M: 好。所以你要一雙白色運動鞋和一件紅條紋 T 恤。）

W: Yes. Here is the money.（W: 是的。錢在這裡。）

25. The woman wants to buy a pair of <u>sports</u> shoes.
   那個女人要買一雙運動鞋。

26. The <u>black</u> pair is 200 dollars.
   <u>黑色的</u>那一雙要價兩百元。

27. The white pair <u>fits</u> the woman well.
   白色的那一雙很<u>適合</u>那個女人。

28. The white pair is <u>150</u> dollars.
   白色的那一雙要<u>一百五十元</u>。

29. The woman likes the T-shirt with red <u>stripes</u>.
   那個女人喜歡有紅色<u>條紋</u>的 T 恤。

30. The woman will pay <u>230</u> dollars for them.
   那個女人要花<u>兩百三十元</u>。

Unit 11

I、Listen and choose the right picture.（根據你所聽到的內容，選出相應的圖片。）（6分）

A.　　　　　　　B.　　　　　　　C.

D.　　　　　E.　　　　　F.　　　　　G.

1. Most of the school students like to play computer games very much.
   （大部分的學校學生非常喜歡玩電腦遊戲。）

   答案：(E)

2. Mr. Li is talking something with his workmate.
   （Li 先生正在與他的同事談事情。）

   答案：(B)

3. The train runs through the tunnel for eight kilometers.
   （火車通過一個八公里的隧道。）

   答案：(F)

4. There is much more rain this year than last year.
   （今年的雨比去年多。）

   答案：(C)

5. Can you make a beautiful kite for my daughter?
   （你能為你女兒做一個漂亮的風箏嗎？）

   答案：(D)

6. People usually light some firecrackers during the Spring Festival.
（人們常常在春假放炮竹。）
答案：(G)

Ⅱ、**Listen and choose the best response to the sentence you hear.**（根據你所聽到的句子，選出最恰當的應答句。）（6分）

7. Would you like to join us to have a picnic in that small country park?
（你想加入我們去那個小型鄉村公園野餐嗎？）
(A)Yes, I'd like to. （是的，我想。）
(B)You're welcome. （不客氣。）
(C)Yes, I will go with you. （是的，我要跟你們去。）
(D)I want to join you. （我想加入你們。）
答案：(A)

8. What did you do last Saturday, Jane?
（Jane，上星期六你做了甚麼？）
(A)I was in the Century Park. （我在中央公園。）
(B)I did some shopping on Friday. （我星期五去購物。）
(C)I visited People's Square. （我參觀了人民廣場。）
(D)My father drove me there. （我父親開車載我去那兒。）
答案：(C)

9. Scientists said that computers would do all the things for us in the future.
（科學家說未來電腦將為我們做所有的事。）
(A)That's wonderful. （那太棒了。）
(B)That's all. （就是這樣。）
(C)All right. （好的。）
(D)That's OK. （好的。）
答案：(A)

10. Would you like to show me how to surf the Internet?
（你能為我展示怎麼瀏覽網際網路嗎？）
(A)I'll be glad to. （我很樂意。）
(B)Yes, I agree. （是的，我同意。）
(C)I'd like to. （我想做。）
(D)Yes, I'd love to. （好，我很樂意。）

答案：(D)

11. My parents are not familiar with the pop stars at all.
（我爸媽對流行明星一點也不熟悉。）
(A)So do mine.（我爸媽也熟悉。）
(B)Neither do mine.（我爸媽也不熟悉。）
(C)So are mine.（我爸媽也是。）
(D)Neither are mine.（我爸媽也是不熟悉。）
答案：(D)

12. Pass me that bottle of shampoo, please.
（請遞給我那瓶洗髮精。）
(A)It's yours.（那是你的。）
(B)Here you are.（給你，在這裡。）
(C)Here we are.（我們到了。）
(D)Help yourself.（自己拿。）
答案：(B)

Ⅲ、Listen to the dialogue and choose the best answer to the question you hear.（根據你所聽到的對話和問題，選出最恰當的答案。）（6分）

13. W: People and animals live on land. Only a quarter of the earth is land.
（W: 人類與動物住在陸地上。地球上只有四分之一是陸地。）
M: Fish and plenty of other sea animals live in water. They live in the streams, rivers, lakes and oceans.
（M: 魚類和其他多種海洋動物住在水裡。它們住在溪流、河流、湖泊和海洋。）
Question: What is three quarters of the earth?
（問題：地球的四分之三是甚麼？）
(A)Water.（水。）
(B)People.（人類。）
(C)Animals.（動物。）
(D)Land.（陸地。）
答案：(A)

14. M: This is a picture of my family.
（M: 這是我家的照片。）
W: Yes, I can see your grandma, your dad, your mum and your dog and this is

you.

（W：是，可以看到你奶奶、你爸爸、你媽媽和你的狗。而這個人是你。）

Question: Who is not in the picture?

（問題：誰不在照片裡？）

(A)My pet.（我的寵物。）

(B)My grandma.（我的奶奶。）

(C)My grandpa.（我的爺爺。）

(D)My parents.（我的父母。）

答案：(C)

15. W: Look, how beautiful the mountains are!

（W：看，這些山多漂亮啊！）

M: Yes. So are the lakes and trees. Shall we have a barbecue here?

（M：是啊。湖泊和樹木也很漂亮。我們可以在這裡烤肉嗎？）

W: Good idea!

（W：好主意！）

Question: Where does the dialogue take place?

（問題：這段對話在哪裡發生？）

(A)At home.（在家。）

(B)At school.（在學校。）

(C)In Pudong.（在浦東。）

(D)In the countryside.（在鄉下。）

答案：(D)

16. W: There is an old man and an old woman next door.

（W：隔壁有一位老先生和一位老婦人。）

M: How do you like them?

（M：你覺得他們怎麼樣？）

W: The old man looks serious and I've never seen him smile. The old lady is very kind.

（W：老先生看起來很嚴肅，我從來沒看他笑過。老太太非常和藹可親。）

Question: Why does the girl say the old man looks serious?

（問題：那個女孩為什麼說老先生看起來很嚴肅？）

(A)He never smiles.（他從不笑。）

(B)She often helps us.（她常幫助我們。）

(C)He is kind to us.（他對我們很好。）

(D)She is a kind lady.（她是一位和善的女士。）

答案：(A)

17. W: Do Dick and Terry do well in the diving?
   （W: Dick 和 Terry 很會潛水嗎？）

   M: Yes. But Lucy does better than them.
   （M: 是的。但是 Lucy 比她們更好。）

   W: What about May?
   （W: May 呢？）

   M: She is the worst of all.
   （M: 她是最糟的。）

   Question: Who does best in the diving?
   （問題：誰最會潛水？）

   (A)Dick.

   (B)May.

   (C)Terry.

   (D)Lucy.

   答案：(D)

18. W: Hurry up. It's time for the English news program. It's on Channel 14.
   （W: 快一點。現在是英語新聞節目的時間了。在第十四頻道。）

   M: Don't worry. There is still a little time to go. Let's finish watching Animal
   World first.
   （M: 別擔心。還有一點時間。我們先看完動物世界吧。）

   W: All right. But don't forget it.
   （W: 好。但是別忘了。）

   M: OK.
   （M: 好。）

   Question: What program are they going to watch?
   （問題：他們要看甚麼節目？）

   (A)Music.（音樂。）

   (B)Animal World.（動物世界。）

   (C)Sports news.（運動新聞。）

   (D)English news.（英語新聞。）

   答案：(D)

Countries around the world have national holidays.

（全世界的國家都有國慶日。）

Of course, the holidays are on different days.

（當然，國慶日是在不同的日子。）

The ways people celebrate national holidays are sometimes the same.

（人們慶祝國慶日的方法常常是一樣的。）

In the United States, the national holiday is on July fourth.

（美國的國慶日是七月四日。）

There are many parades.

（有非常多的遊行。）

People cook food outside and eat outdoors.

（人們在戶外料理食物也在戶外吃東西。）

In France, the national holiday is on July fourteenth.

（法國的國慶日是七月十四日。）

There are big parades, and airplanes fly overhead in the sky.

（有大型遊行，飛機群飛越天空。）

People dance in the streets.

（人們在街上跳舞。）

Many events such as concerts and films are free on that day.

（有非常多像音樂會和影片放映之類的活動，當天都是免費的。）

Mexican Independence Day is on May fifth.

（墨西哥獨立日在五月五日。）

There are big parades, too.

（也有大型遊行。）

In Mexico City, people put on a play: it shows how Mexico won its independence.

（人們在墨西哥市上演一齣戲劇：它展示了墨西哥如何贏得它的獨立。）

And everywhere there are mariachi music, and dancing in the streets.

（每個地方的街道上都有墨西哥街頭音樂（瑪麗亞西）和舞蹈。）

Many people eat a favorite Mexican dish, Mole poblano（chicken made with chocolate）, on this day.

（許多人在當天吃著最受歡迎的墨西哥菜「Mole poblano」（巧克力牛肉）。）

19. The national holidays in different countries are on the same day.

（不同國家的國慶日都在同一天。）

答案：（F 錯）

20. Mexico's Independence Day is on July 14.
（墨西哥獨立日在七月十四日。）

答案：（F 錯）

21. In the United States, people have parades on July 4.
（在美國，人們在七月四日有遊行活動。）

答案：（T 對）

22. In France, you don't need to pay money if you go to the concerts on their national holiday.
（在法國，如果你在國慶日參加音樂會就不需要付錢。）

答案：（T 對）

23. In France, people play mariachi music on Independence Day.
（在法國，人們在獨立日演奏墨西哥街頭音樂(瑪麗亞西)。）

答案：（F 錯）

24. In the United States, France and Mexico, there are parades for Independence Day.
（美國、法國、墨西哥在獨立日都有遊行。）

答案：（T 對）

Ⅴ、Listen to the dialogue and complete the table.（根據你所聽到的對話內容，用適當的單詞或數字完成下面的表格。每空格限填一詞或數字，或在方框內打勾。）（6分）

Shopping 購物

M: Good morning, Madam. What can I do for you?
（M: 女士，早安。我能為你服務嗎？）

W: I want to buy a pair of sports shoes of size 8.
（W: 我想要買一雙尺寸是八號的運動鞋。）

M: What about the black one? It's 200 dollars.
（M: 黑色的這雙怎麼樣？要兩百元。）

W: It's smart but too expensive. Can you show me another pair?
（W: 那太小了而且太貴。你能給我看看另一雙嗎？）

M: The white pair is nice. Will you try it on?
（M: 白色的那一雙不錯。你要試試看嗎。）

W: Yes, it fits me very well. How much then?

（W: 好。它非常適合我。多少錢呢？）

M: 50 cheaper.

（M: 便宜 50 元。）

W: All right. I'll take it. By the way, how much is the T-shirt of size 12?

（W: 好。我買了。附帶提一下，尺寸十二號的 T 恤多少錢？）

M: The red one is 80 dollars, the blue one is 40 dollars.

（M: 紅色的八十元，藍色的四十元。）

W: All right. I'll take the red one. Here's the money.

（W: 好。我要買紅色的。錢在這裡。）

Things to buy （要買的東西）	a pair of __25__ shoes （一雙＿＿鞋）	a T-shirt （一件T恤）
Size （尺寸）	Size 8 （八號）	Size 26 （二十六號）
The colour she likes （她喜歡的顏色）	__27__ Black □ White □ （＿＿ 黑色 □ 白色 □）	Red ☑ Blue □ （紅色☑黑色 □）
Price （價格）	The black one $__28__ （黑色的＿＿元） The white one __29__ （白色的＿＿元）	The red one $80 （紅色的八十元） The blue one $40 （藍色的四十元）
How much to pay altogether （一共付了多少錢）	$__30__ （＿＿元）	

25. 答案：Sports (運動)

26. 答案：12

27. 答案：White ☑ (白色的)

28. 答案：200

29. 答案：150

30. 答案：230

全新國中會考英語聽力精選(中)原文及參考答案

Unit 12

A.　　B.　　C.

D.　　E.　　F.　　G.

1. Do you still play with lanterns on Lantern Festival in your town?
   (在你的城市你們仍然在元宵節玩燈籠嗎?)
   答案:(F)

2. There are many passengers waiting for the light rail train at the station.
   (有很多旅客在車站等待輕軌列車。)
   答案:(C)

3. How about having a picnic this coming Saturday? (即將來到的這個星期六舉辦個野餐如何?)
   答案:(E)

4. The students are talking about their trip to the Palace Museum happily.
   (學生們正快樂地談論著他們去故宮博物院的旅行。)
   答案:(B)

5. Finally, their little sister burst into laughter after her brother and sister tried for a long time.
   (終於,在哥哥姊姊們試了好久之後他們的小妹笑了出來。)
   答案:(D)

6. Stop making noise, guys! Mr Lin is coming! (停止製造噪音,哥兒們!林先生來了!)
   答案:(G)

II、Listen to the dialogue and choose the best answer to the question you

hear.

7. W: Hello, Tom. What are you busy doing over there? (女：哈囉，湯姆。你在那邊忙什麼？)

    M: I'm carrying a box to the classroom. (男：我正在把一個盒子搬到教室去。)

    W: What's in the box? (女：那盒子裡有什麼？)

    M: Some books and magazines. (男：一些書和雜誌。)

    W: Do you need some help? (女：你需要幫忙嗎？)

    M: No, thanks. I can manage. (男：不，謝謝。我能搞定。)

    Question: What does Tom mean? (問題：湯姆的意思是什麼？)

    (A)He can carry the box. (他搬得動那盒子。)

    (B)The box is very heavy. (盒子很重。)

    (C)Tom needs some help. (湯姆需要幫忙。)

    (D)He can't carry the box. (他搬不動盒子。)

    答案：(A)

8. M: What did you do last night? (男：妳昨晚做了什麼？)

    W: I studied English. And I watched TV at the same time.(女：我讀英文。同時我還看了電視。)

    M: How could you do that? (男：妳怎麼做得到？)

    W: It was very easy. The film on TV was in English.
       (女：很簡單。電視所播出的電影是英文的。)

    M: Well done. I'll try next time, too. (男：做得好。下次我也來試試。)

    Question: What did the girl do last night? (問題：這位女生昨晚做了什麼？)

    (A)She studied English and then watched TV. (她先讀英文再看電視。)

    (B)She studied English instead of watching TV. (她讀英文沒有看電視。)

    (C)She watched TV after she studied English. (她看完電視後讀英文。)

    (D)She studied English by watching TV. (她看電視學英文。)

    答案：(D)

9. W: Hi, Tom. Where are you going? (女：嗨，湯姆。你要去哪裡？)

    M: I'm going to the cinema. What time is it by your watch?
       (男：我正要去電影院。妳的手錶幾點？)

    W: It's half past two. (女：兩點半。)

    M: Oh! There are only fifteen minutes left. My watch is ten minutes slow. I must hurry.
       See you later. (男：噢！只剩下十五分鐘了。我的手錶慢了十分鐘。我得趕快。
       回頭見。)

    Question: What time will the film begin? (問題：電影幾時將開演？)

    (A)2.30.   (B)2.40.   (C)2.45.   (D)3.00.

    答案：(C)

10. M: Where had you lived before you moved to Shanghai? (男：妳搬到上海之前住在哪

裡？)

    W: In Nanjing. (女：在南京。)

    M: I went to Nanjing last summer. I don't like it. It's too hot in summer.
      (男：去年夏天我去了南京。我不喜歡。那邊夏天太熱了。)

    W: Oh, I do. There are more trees there than here.
      (女：喔，我挺喜歡的。那邊比這邊有更多樹木。)

    M: But why have you moved here? (男：但是妳為什麼搬過來這邊？)

    W: I have got a better job in Shanghai. (女：我在上海得到一個較好的工作。)

    Question: Who likes Nanjing? (問題：誰喜歡南京？)

    (A)The man. (男士)   (B)The woman. (女士)

    (C)Both of them. (都喜歡)   (D)Neither of them. (都不喜歡)

    答案：(B)

11. W: It's a pity! The film was just over. Tom, where have you been?
      (女：好可惜！電影剛結束。湯姆，你去了哪裡啊？)

    M: I've been to school. Professor Yang made a speech this morning.
      (男：我去了學校。楊教授今天早上發表了一場演講。)

    W: Really? What was it about? (女：真的？是講什麼的？)

    M: It was about space science. It's very interesting. (男：是講太空科學的。很有意思。)

    W: I'm interested in space science, too. (女：我也對太空科學有興趣。)

    Question: Why did the boy go to school? (問題：這位男生為什麼去學校？)

    (A)To have a talk. (去談話。)   (B)To have an English lesson. (上英文課。)

    (C)To attend a lecture. (去聽演講。)   (D)To play football. (去踢足球。)

    答案：(C)

12. M: Hi! Jane. What are you doing now? (男：嗨！珍。妳現在正在做什麼？)

    W: I'm reading a book. Could you tell me what this word means?
      (女：我正在讀一本書。你可以告訴我這個字的意義嗎？)

    M: Sorry, I don't know its meaning. (男：抱歉，我不知道它的意義。)

    W: What can I do? (女：我能怎麼辦？)

    M: Why not look it up in the dictionary? I have got a good dictionary.
      (男：何不在字典裡查一查？我有一本好字典。)

    W: Good idea. (女：好主意。)

    Question: What are they going to do soon? (問題：他們即將做什麼？)

    (A)To buy a dictionary. (買字典)

    (B)To look up the word in the dictionary. (在字典裡查那個單字)

    (C)To borrow a dictionary. (借字典)

    (D)To ask the teacher for help. (請老師幫忙)

    答案：(B)

13. W: What time is it now? (女：現在幾點？)

M: About half past four. It's still early. (男：大約四點半。還早。)

W: I'm afraid I must go now. (女：我恐怕必須現在離開。)

M: Why are you in such a hurry? Can't you stay for supper?

(男：妳為何如此匆忙？妳不能留下來用晚餐嗎？)

W: Thank you for your kindness, but I must buy some vegetables for supper before my son comes home from school.

(女：謝謝你的好意，但我必須在我兒子從學校回家之前買些晚餐要吃的蔬菜。)

Question: Where is the woman going now? (問題：這位女士現在要去哪裡？)

(A)To her office. (去辦公室)

(B)To school. (去學校)

(C)To the market. (去市場)

(D)To stay for supper. (在家做晚餐)

答案：(C)

14. M: Hi, Mary. I hear your school library is very large. Can you tell me something about it?

(男：嗨，瑪莉。我聽說妳學校的圖書館很大。妳可以告訴我一些關於它的事嗎？)

W: Certainly. What would you like to know? (女：當然。你想知道些什麼？)

M: How many books have you got? (男：你們有多少本書？)

W: About 40,000 altogether. Some are Chinese, and others are English.

(女：總共大約四萬本。有些是中文的，而其它是英文的。)

M: How many English books? (男：有多少英文書？)

W: About a quarter of the total. (女：大約總數的四分之一。)

Question: How many English books are there in the school's library?

(問題：在此校的圖書館裡有多少本英文書？)

(A)40,000.　　　　(B)30,000.　　　　(C)20,000.　　　　(D)10,000.

答案：(D)

15. M: I'd like to eat some chocolate, Mum. (男：我想要吃些巧克力，媽媽。)

W: I'm afraid you can't. You always have too much of it. It's bad for your teeth.

(女：我恐怕你不行喔。你總是吃太多。它對你的牙齒不好。)

M: But I will brush my teeth before going to bed. (男：但是我在睡前會刷牙啊。)

W: You'll become fatter and fatter. (女：你將會變得愈來愈胖。)

M: What else can I eat then? (男：那麼還有什麼其它我可以吃的？)

W: You'd better eat more fruit and vegetables. They are good for your health.

(女：你最好多吃些水果和蔬菜。它們對你的健康有益。)

Question: What does the boy usually like to eat? (問題：這個男孩通常喜歡吃什麼？)

(A)Some chicken. (雞肉)　　　　　　　(B)Some chocolate. (巧克力)

(C)Some fruit. (水果)　　　　　　　　　　(D)Some vegetables.

(蔬菜)

答案：(B)

16. W: Mike, you didn't come to school yesterday. Was there anything wrong?

  （女：麥克，你昨天沒來學校。有什麼狀況嗎？）

  M: Yes, I had a bad cold. The doctor told me to stay in bed for at least one day.

  （男：有，我重感冒。醫師要我至少在床上待一天。）

  W: I'm sorry to hear that. How are you today? （女：我很遺憾聽到這消息。你今天如何？）

  M: Much better, thank you. The headmaster told me you gave the lessons to my students yesterday. It's very kind of you.

  （男：好多了，謝謝。校長告訴我妳昨天幫我的學生上了課。妳真好心。）

  W: It's my pleasure. （女：我很樂意的。）

  Question: What is Mike? （問題：麥克的職業是？）

  (A)The doctor. (醫生)   (B)The headmaster. (主任)

  (C)The teacher. (老師)   (D)The student. (學生)

  答案：(C)

Ⅲ、Listen to the passage and decide whether the following statements are True (T) or False (F).

You will love beautiful San Francisco!

你會愛上美麗的舊金山！

San Francisco Bay is a harbour of bright blue water. To look down on the bay, travel up the highest hill by cable car. Of course, you can also walk, but you will need strong legs! It is never too hot and never too cold here. Sports-lovers can come and watch American football or baseball games. Food-lovers will find delicious fish and other seafood at our great restaurants.

舊金山灣是個有湛藍海水的港口。要俯瞰海灣，就搭纜車上最高的山丘。當然，你也可以徒步，但你會需要強壯的雙腿！這裡的天氣從不會太熱也從不會太冷。運動愛好者可以來觀賞美式足球或棒球賽。美食愛好者可以在我們絕讚的餐廳裡找到美味的魚和其他海鮮。

Enjoy the California sunshine!

享受加州的陽光！

See the famous Golden Gate Bridge. Cross the bridge to Golden Gate Park, with its beautiful lakes, trees and gardens. In the park you can fish, walk or play tennis. When you need a rest, come and have something to eat and drink in our Japanese Tea Garden. Nothing could be nicer!

看看著名的金門大橋。過橋到金門公園，它有著美麗的湖泊、樹和花園。在公園裡你可以釣魚、散步或打網球。當你需要休息，來我們的日本茶花園吃喝點東西吧。沒有更棒的事了！

Spend Chinese New Year's Day

歡度中國新年

Here! For a Chinese New Year's Day with a difference, come to San Francisco and take part in our wonderful festival. San Francisco's Chinatown is the largest outside Asia. Behind its big green gate, you will find all kinds of food from China, and many warm welcomes.

來！想度過一個與眾不同的中國新年，來舊金山參加我們精彩的慶典。舊金山的中國城是在亞洲以外最大規模的。在它巨大的綠色大門後，你將找到各種來自中國的食物和許多熱烈的歡迎。

17. San Francisco is a cold, dark place.(舊金山是個寒冷、陰暗的地方。)

答案：(F 錯)

18. According to the passage, it is a long way to walk to the top of the hill if you want to look down on San Francisco Bay.(根據此文，如果你想俯瞰舊金山灣的話徒步上山丘頂的路很長。)

答案：(T 對)

19. Only sports-lovers or food-lovers should visit San Francisco.(只有運動愛好者或美食愛好者該造訪舊金山。)

答案：(T 對)

20. Golden Gate Park is near Golden Gate Bridge.(金門公園靠近金門大橋。)

答案：(T 對)

21. You can find a Japanese Tea Garden in the Golden Gate Park.

(你可以在金門公園內找到日本茶花園。)

答案：(T 對)

22. In Chinatown you can only get hot Sichuan food. (在中國城你只能買到辣的四川料理。)

答案：(F 錯)

23. San Francisco's Chinatown is bigger than London's. (舊金山的中國城比倫敦的更大。)

答案：(T 對)

Ⅳ、Listen to the passage and fill in the blanks.

Today, I am going to talk about Bangkok, my hometown and the capital of my country, Thailand. There are many interesting places to visit in Bangkok, but first I want to tell you about our traffic problem.

今天，我將和大家談談曼谷，我的家鄉並且是我國泰國的首都。曼谷有很多可參觀的有趣所在，但首先我想告訴各位關於我們的交通問題。

The streets are very crowded in Bangkok, so it can take a long time to get from place to place. It used to take me more than two hours to get to school by bus! I often slept on my way there!

在曼谷的街道非常擁擠，所以從一處到另一處可能要很長時間。我曾經需要花超過兩小時搭公車上學！在那邊我經常在路途中睡覺！

If you want to get somewhere on time in Bangkok, you must leave early. Lots of people take tuk-tuks to get through the traffic quickly. Tuk-tuks are like little cars with three wheels.

如果你想在曼谷準時到達某處，你必須提早出發。很多人搭嘟嘟車快速通過塞車。嘟嘟車像有三個輪子的小汽車。

Bangkok is next to a big river. It is interesting to visit the Floating Market on the river. At the market, people sell lots of fresh fruit and vegetables from their boats.

曼谷緊鄰一條大河。參觀河上的水上市場很有趣。在市場裡，人們從他們的船上販賣大量的新鮮水果和蔬菜。

In November, we have the Festival of Lights. Everyone makes lights during the festival. Then, after dark, we put them carefully into the river and watch them sail away. It is beautiful to see the river with millions of little lights on it.

十一月時，我們有點燈節。在此節日每個人都製作燈飾。接著，天黑後，我們小心地把它們放到河裡看著它們漂走。看著河上百萬盞小燈光很美。

Thailand is also famous for its food. Thai food is very hot like some Chinese food. So if you like Sichuan food, you'll love Thai food!

泰國也以它的美食著名。泰式料理像一些中國料理一樣很辣。所以如果你喜歡四川菜，你也會愛上泰國菜！

Many thanks, everyone, for listening to me.

多謝各位聽我講述。

- Streets in Bangkok are __24__
  (曼谷的街道擁擠。)
- People must leave __25__ if they go to work in the morning.
  (如果他們早上去上班，人們必須提早出發。)
- Tuk-tuks are like little __26__ with __27__ wheels
  (嘟嘟車像有三個輪子的小汽車。)
- Bangkok is famous for its Floating __28__
  (曼谷以它的水上市場而著名。)
- People sell fruit and vegetables from their __29__
  (人們從他們的船上販賣水果和蔬菜。)
- Thai food are usually very __30__
  (泰國料理通常很辣。)

24. 答案：crowded (擁擠)
25. 答案：early (早)
26. 答案：cars (汽車)
27. 答案：three/3 (三)
28. 答案：Market (市場)
29. 答案：boats (船)
30. 答案：hot (辣)

Unit 13

I、Listen and choose the right picture.（根據你所聽到的內容,選出相應的圖片。）（6分）

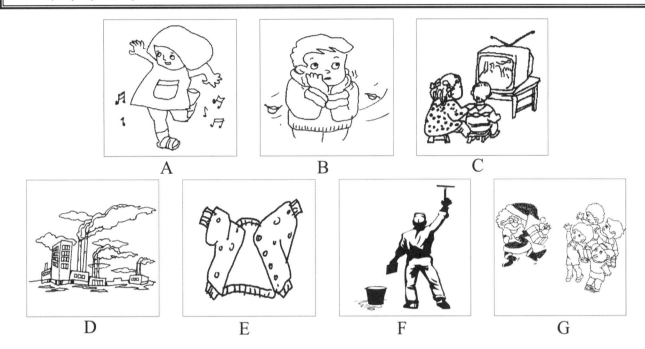

A   B   C

D   E   F   G

1. On Christmas Day little children hope to get presents from Santa Claus.
   （小朋友希望在聖誕節得到聖誕老人的禮物。）

   答案：(G)

2. I'd like to buy a sweater with spots.（我想買一件有點點花紋的毛衣）

   答案：(E)

3. John managed to paint the walls himself at home.
   （John 計畫在家裡自己油漆牆壁。）

   答案：(F)

4. The wind blows fiercely and the leaves start falling from the tree. Autumn is coming.
   （風猛烈地吹，葉子開始從樹上掉落。秋天就要來了。）

   答案：(B)

5. The air pollution is getting more and more serious in some developing countries.（空氣汙染在某些開發中國家變得越來越嚴重了。）

   答案：(D)

6. We watched the final of the FIFA World Cup 2010 excitedly at home.
（我們在家興奮地觀看二零一零年世界杯足球賽的總決賽。）
答案：(C)

II、**Listen and choose the best response to the sentence you hear.（根據你所聽到的句子,選出最恰當的應答句。）（6分）**

7. My ambition is to be an architect.（我的志向是當一名建築師。）
(A)So do mine.（我的也是。） (B)Neither do mine.（我的也不是。）
(C)So is mine.（我的也是。） (D)Neither is mine.（我的也不是。）
答案：(C)

8. Could you turn down the radio a bit?（你把收音機轉小聲一點好嗎？）
(A)Yes, I can.（是的，我可以。）
(B)No, I can't.（不，我不可以。）
(C)I'm sorry to have bothered you.（很抱歉打擾到你了。）
(D)Yes, I could.（是的，我可以。）
答案：(C)

9. May I speak to Mr. Brown?（請 Brown 先生聽電話好嗎？）
(A)Yes, I am.（是的，我是。） (B)Yes, he is.（是，他是。）
(C)Yes, speaking.（我就是。） (D)I'm Mr. Brown.（我是 Brown 先生。）
答案：(C)

10. Many trees fell down in the typhoon last week.
（許多樹在上星期的颱風中傾倒了。）
(A)What a pity!（好可惜。） (B)What fun!（好有趣！）
(C)I know.（我知道。） (D)I don't think so.（我不這麼認為。）
答案：(A)

11. Could you leave a message?（請你留言好嗎？）
(A)Certainly.（當然。） (B)That's all right.（沒關係。）
(C)That's right.（對的。） (D)You're welcome.（不客氣。）
答案：(A)

12. How often do you brush your teeth every day?（你每天刷幾次牙？）
(A)In a day.（一天內。） (B)Twice a day.（一天兩次。）
(C)At 7 o'clock.（七點。） (D)For two times.（兩次。）
答案：(B)

13. W: Can I help you, sir?（W: 先生,我能為你服務嗎?）

M: Sure. Is your library open on Saturday?（M: 嗯。你們的圖書館星期天開放嗎?）

W: No. It's open from Monday to Friday. We don't work at the weekend.

（W: 不開放。星期一到星期五開放。我們周末不上班。）

Q: When can people borrow books from the library?

（Q: 人們甚麼時候可以到圖書館借書?）

(A)At the weekend.（周末。）　　　　(B)On weekdays.（平日。）

(C)On Saturday.（星期六。）　　　　(D)On Sunday.（星期天。）

答案：(B)

14. W: May I speak to John, please?（W: 請找 John 聽電話好嗎?）

M: Sorry, you've got the wrong number.（M: 抱歉,你打錯號碼了。）

W: Is that 6627594?（W: 是 6627594 嗎?）

M: No. It's 6624594.（M: 不。這裡是 6624594。）

Q: What's John's telephone number?（Q: John 的電話號碼是幾號?）

(A)6624594.　　(B)6627594.　　(C)6627495.　　(D)6624495.

答案：(B)

15. W: How lovely you were! How old were you then?

（W: 你真可愛!那時候你幾歲?）

M: I was three years old. My aunt took the photo. She likes children very much.

（M: 我三歲。我阿姨拍的相片。她非常喜歡小孩。）

Q: What are they doing?（Q: 他們在做甚麼?）

(A)They are looking at the photo.（他們在看相片。）

(B)They are visiting a kindergarten.（他們在參觀幼稚園。）

(C)They are talking to an aunt.（她們在跟一位阿姨說話。）

(D)They are watching TV.（他們在看電視。）

答案：(A)

16. W: Peter, what can we use water for?（W: Peter,我們可以拿水來做甚麼?）

M: Sorry, Miss Wu, I'm not quite sure.)（M: Wu 小姐,很抱歉,我不大確定。）

W: You'd better work harder. Sit down, please. Who can help Peter?

（W: 你最好努力一點。請坐下。誰能來幫 Peter?）

Q: What is Miss Wu?（Q: Wu 小姐是做甚麼的?）

(A)A student.（學生。）　　　　(B)A nurse.（護士。）

(C)A teacher.（老師。）　　　　(D)A doctor.（醫生。）

答案：(C)

17. W: When will our plane leave?（W: 我們的飛機何時離開？）

    M: At 10:45 tomorrow morning. But we have to arrive at the airport two hours earlier.

    （M: 明天早上十點四十五分。但是我們要提早兩小時到機場。）

    Q: When must they get to the airport?（Q: 他們必須何時抵達機場？）

    (A)10:45.（十點四十五分。）　　　　(B)9:45.（九點四十五分。）

    (C)11:45.（十一點四十五分。）　　　(D)8:45.（八點四十五分。）

    答案：(D)

18. W: Do you want me to get you anything? I'm leaving now.

    （W: 你要我幫你買東西嗎？我現在要走了。）

    M: I want three loaves of bread and two kilos of apples.

    （M: 我要三條麵包和兩公斤蘋果。）

    W: Okay. I will get them.（W: 好。我會去買。）

    Q: Where is the girl going?（Q: 女孩要去哪裡？）

    (A)To a post office.（郵局。）　　　　(B)To a food shop.（食品店。）

    (C)To a library.（圖書館。）　　　　(D)To a bank.（銀行。）

    答案：(B)

IV、Listen to the dialogue and decide whether the following statements are True (T) or False (F).（判斷下列句子內容是否符合你所聽到的對話內容,符合的用"T"表示,不符合的用"F"表示。）（6分）

Forests are very important to men and animals. They provide food and shelters for animals. If there are no trees, animals will have no food or shelters. They will soon die. We get many materials from forests. We get food from trees. Wood is useful for making paper and furniture. Land is also important. We use oil to make plastic. We use metal to make cans and use clay for making bowls and plates. We get sand from beaches. We use sand to make glass. All the things we get from forests and land are necessary in our daily life. We can't live without forests or land. Everyone should protect forests and our environment.

森林對人類和動物來說非常重要。森林為動物提供了食物和藏匿之處。如果沒有了樹木，動物將沒有食物和藏匿之處。牠們很快就會死亡。我們從森林取得很多素材。我們從樹木中取得食物。木材可以用來製作紙張和家具。陸地也很重要。我們利用石油來製作塑膠。用金屬來製作罐頭，用黏土來製作碗盤。我們從海灘取得沙子。我們利用沙子來做玻璃。我們從森林與陸地取得的所有東西，在我們的日常生活中都是必要的。沒有了森林或陸地我們將不能生存。每個人都應該保護森林與我們的環境。

19. Forests are important to us.（森林對我們很重要。）

    答案：(T 對)

20. Trees only provide food for animals.（樹木只能為動物提供食物。）

    答案：(F 錯)

21. Animals will die quickly without trees. （沒有了樹木，動物很快就會死亡 。）

    答案：(T 對)

22. Cans are made of clay. （罐頭是黏土做的。）

    答案：(F 錯)

23. Glass is made from sand on the beaches. （玻璃是由海灘的沙所製成的。）

    答案：(T 對)

24. Everything we use in our daily life comes from trees and land.
    （我們日常生活中所使用的每一件東西都來自樹木和陸地。）

    答案：(F 錯)

Ⅴ、Listen and fill in the blanks.（根據你所聽到的內容,用適當的單詞完成下面的句子。每空格限填一詞。）（6分）

M: Hello, Lingling, you look so sad and worried.
（M: 哈囉 Lingling，妳看起來很難過、很擔心的樣子。）

W: Yes. I think all of us feel sad these days because of the mudslide from the mountain in early August, in Gansu.
（W: 是的。這幾天我們大家都因為八月上旬在甘肅山區發生的土石流而感到難過。）

M: Yes, it was terrible. Many people were hurt. About 1,300 people died.
（M: 是的，那真的很可怕。許多人受傷了。大約一千三百人死亡。）

W: Many children lost their parents, and many parents lost their children. Most of them lost their homes. Students there can't go to school.
（W: 許多孩子失去了父母，許多父母失去了孩子。他們大部分都失去了家園。學生們沒辦法上學。）

M: This is the worst news of the year. But what can we do to help them?
（M: 這是今年最糟的消息。然而，我們能做些甚麼來幫助他們呢？）

W: Just now we had a class meeting. We've decided to raise some money for them. We are going to buy some books, schoolbags, pens, rulers and something else for them. （W: 就在剛才我們開了一次班級會議。我們決定為他們募捐。我們要買書、書包、筆、尺和其他物品給他們。）

M: That's great. My dad is an architect. He is going to help the people to rebuild their homes.
（M:太棒了。我爸爸是建築師。他要幫助他們重建家園。）

W: I hope everything will go well with them. （W: 我希望他們能事事順利。）

M: I hope so, too. （M: 我也這麼希望。）

25. The mudslide happened in early <u>August</u> in Gansu.
    甘肅的土石流發生在<u>八月</u>上旬。

26. Many people were <u>hurt</u>.
許多人<u>受傷</u>。

27. About <u>1,300</u> people died.
大約<u>一千三百</u>人死亡。

28. We had a class <u>meeting</u> just now.
我們剛才有個班級<u>會議</u>。

29. We've decided to <u>raise</u> some money for them.
我們決定為他們<u>募捐</u>。

30. The boy's father is an <u>architect</u>.
男孩的父親是<u>建築師</u>。

全新國中會考英語聽力精選(中)原文及參考答案

Unit 14

I、Listen and choose the right picture.

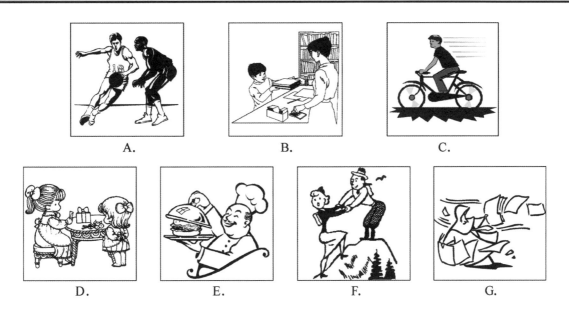

1. Hey, my dear. We finally reached the top of the mountain. What a nice view we have here!
   (嘿，親愛的。我們終於到達山頂了。這裡的風景真棒！)
   答案：(F)

2. Here's a card and my present for you, Jane. I hope you will like it.
   (這是一張卡片和我給妳的禮物，珍。我希望妳會喜歡它。)
   答案：(D)

3. Miss, may I take these two books home? (小姐，我可以把這兩本書帶回家嗎？)
   答案：(B)

4. My grandfather used to be a cook at the Park Hotel. (我祖父曾經是公園飯店的廚師。)
   答案：(E)

5. What a terrible day! I even can't walk in the wind. (多麼糟的天氣！在風中我甚至走不動。)
   答案：(G)

6. What's your plan for Sunday, Tom? How about having a basketball match with the students from Class 3?
   (你星期天的計劃是什麼，湯姆？和三班的學生們打一場籃球賽如何？)
   答案：(A)

7.　W: Shall we meet at the school gate at 2.00 in the afternoon?
　　　（女：我們要不要下午兩點在學校大門口碰面？）

　　　M: Sorry, I might be late. My piano lesson won't be over till 2.30. Can we meet at 3.00 in the afternoon? (男：抱歉，我可能會遲到。我的鋼琴課直到兩點半才會結束。我們可以下午三點碰面嗎？)

　　　W: No problem. See you then. (女：沒問題。到時候見。)

　　　Question: What time are they going to meet at the school gate?
　　　（問題：他們將幾點在學校大門碰面？）

　　　(A)At 2.00.　　　(B)At 2.30.　　　(C)At 3.00.　　　(D)At 3.30.
　　　答案：(C)

8.　M: Can I help you, Miss? (男：我可以效勞嗎，小姐？)

　　　W: Well, I'm looking for some CDs for my daughter. She likes S.H.E. best.
　　　（女：好，我正在為我女兒找一些 CD。她最喜歡 S.H.E.）

　　　M: How about this one? It's the latest. (男：這張怎麼樣？它是最新的。)

　　　W: OK. How much is it? (女：好。它多少錢？)

　　　M: 58 yuan. (男：五十八元。)

　　　Question: Where does this dialogue probably take place?
　　　（問題：這段對話可能發生在什麼場所？）

　　　(A)In a library. (在圖書館)　　　　　(B)In a CD shop. (在唱片行)
　　　(C)In a theater. (在電影院)　　　　(D)In a restaurant. (在餐廳)
　　　答案：(B)

9.　W: How do you usually go to school, Mike? (女：你通常怎麼去學校，麥克？)

　　　M: I usually ride a bicycle. But if it rains, I go by bus.
　　　（男：我通常騎腳踏車。但如果下雨，我就搭巴士。）

　　　Question: How does Mike usually go to school? (問題：麥克通常怎麼去學校？)

　　　(A)By bus. (搭公車)　　　　　　　(B)By bike. (騎單車)
　　　(C)On foot. (步行)　(D)By car. (開車)
　　　答案：(B)

10.　W: Would you like to visit Alice with me after school? She's been ill for two days.
　　　（女：你想要放學後和我一起去拜訪艾莉絲嗎？她生病兩天了。）

　　　M: I'm afraid I can't. I have to take care of Mary, my little sister.
　　　（男：我恐怕不行。我必須照顧瑪莉，我妹妹。）

　　　W: That's OK. (女：沒關係。)

　　　Question: Why can't the boy visit Alice with the girl?
　　　（問題：為什麼這位男孩不能和這位女孩去拜訪艾莉絲？）

　　　(A)Because he has to look after his sister. (因為他要照顧妹妹。)

(B)Because he will visit Mary. (因為他要去看 Mary。)

(C)Because he has visited Alice. (因為他已經去看過 Alice 了。)

(D)Because she will visit her. (因為她要去看她)

答案：(A)

11. W: What's in your big bag? (女：你的大袋子裡有什麼？)

　　M: Some food, drinks, a raincoat and some medicine.

　　　（男：一些食物、飲料、一件雨衣和一些藥品。）

　　W: Have you got a camera and enough films? (女：你有一台相機和足夠的底片嗎？)

　　M: Sure. I like taking photos during my trip. (男：當然。我喜歡在我的旅途中拍照。)

　　Question: What's the boy going to do? (問題：這位男孩要去做什麼？)

　　(A)To have a picnic. (去野餐)　　　　　　(B)To take some films. (拍一些影片)

　　(C)To go on a trip. (去旅行)　　　　　　(D)To buy some food. (去買食物)

　　答案：(C)

12. M: Do you like the dishes here? Have you got any suggestions for us?

　　　（男：妳喜歡這裡的料理嗎？妳有任何給我們的建議嗎？）

　　W: Well, the food is very delicious. I think I'll come here again.

　　　（女：嗯，料理很美味。我想我會再次來這裡。）

　　Question: Who are the two speakers? (問題：這兩位對話者是誰？)

　　(A)Mum and son. (媽媽和兒子)　　　　　(B)Teacher and student. (老師和學生)

　　(C)Waiter and customer. (侍者和客人)　　(D)Host and guest. (主人和客人)

　　答案：(C)

13. W: What does your father do, John? (女：你父親的職業是什麼，約翰？)

　　M: He's a doctor, and my Mum is a nurse. They work in the same hospital. I hope I can

　　　be a doctor, too. (男：他是一名醫師，而我媽媽是一名護士。他們在同一間醫院

　　　工作。我希望我也可以成為一名醫師。)

　　W: That's very nice. I hope your dream will come true. (女：那很好。我希望你的夢想

　　　將成真。)

　　Question: What job does the boy's father do? (問題：這位男孩的父親是做什麼職

　　　業？)

　　(A)Dentist. (牙醫)　(B)Nurse. (護士)　　　(C)Teacher. (老師)　　　(D)Doctor. (醫生)

　　答案：(D)

14. M: I've moved to my new flat at the seaside. (男：我搬去我在海邊的新公寓了。)

　　W: What's your new telephone number? (女：你的新電話號碼是幾號？)

　　M: 62580023. (男：62580023.)

　　W: That same as the old one? (女：那是和舊的一樣？)

　　M: No, my old telephone number was 64580023. (男：不，我的舊電話號碼是

　　64580023。)

　　Question: What's the boy's new telephone number? (問題：這位男孩的新電話號碼

(A)64580023.　　　(B)62580023.　　　(C)64850023.　　　(D)62850023.

答案：(B)

15. W: What do you usually have for breakfast on Sundays? (女：你星期天的早餐通常吃什麼？)

M: I usually have coffee and bread. What about you? (男：我通常喝咖啡吃麵包。那妳呢？)

W: I never have breakfast. So I often have a lot for lunch. I like beef and pork.
(女：我從來不吃早餐。所以我常常午餐吃很多。我喜歡牛肉和豬肉。)

Question: What does the woman usually have for breakfast?

(問題：這位女士通常早餐吃什麼？)

(A)Coffee and bread. (咖啡和麵包)　　　(B)Beef and pork. (牛肉和豬肉)

(C)Meat. (肉類)　　　(D)Nothing. (不吃早餐)

答案：(D)

16. W: Can I speak to Tom? (女：我可以和湯姆說話嗎？)

M: This is Tom speaking. (男：我就是湯姆。)

W: Well, this is Jenny. I bought a new computer this morning, but it doesn't work. I wonder if you can come and have a look. (女：喔，我是珍妮。我今天早上買了一台新電腦，但是它不能運作。我不知道你是否可以來看看。)

Question: Where are they talking? (問題：他們在哪裡對話？)

(A)On the phone. (在電話上)　　　(B)At Jenny's home. (在 Jenny 家)

(C)At the computer room. (在電腦室)　　　(D)At Tom's home. (在 Tom 家)

答案：(A)

Ⅲ、Listen to the passage and decide whether the following statements are True (T) or False (F).

I have several questions for you: Do you often see a blue sky above our city? Is the air in our city fresh? Is the water in our river clean? The answers to these questions are all "No"!

我有幾個問題要問你們：你們經常在我們的都市上空看到藍天嗎？我們都市的空氣新鮮嗎？我們河流中的水乾淨嗎？這些問題的答案都是「不」！

My grandfather often tells many interesting stories about his childhood. At that time, the sky was blue, the air was fresh and the water was clean. When my grandfather and his friends played in the forest, they could hear birds sing. When they swam in the river, they could see many fish. It was a happy time.

我的祖父經常講很多關於他童年的有趣故事。在那時候，天空是藍的，空氣是新鮮的而且水是乾淨的。當我的祖父和他的朋友們在森林裡玩，他們可以聽到鳥兒在唱歌。當他們在河中游泳，他們可以看到很多魚。那是個快樂的時光。

However, today, the air and water are becoming dirtier. People are killing animals, and cutting down and burning trees. Some animals and plants are now disappearing. The earth is in trouble.

然而，今天，空氣和水變得比較髒。人們殘殺動物，還砍伐且焚燒樹木。有些動物和植物現在正在消失中。這地球陷入麻煩了。

I want you to join us by helping protect our environment. We need to protect Earth because it is our home. We do not need to do big things — we can start out small. Do not throw any rubbish onto the ground. Do not waste water. Use both sides of paper when you write. Stop using plastic bags for shopping.

我希望你們加入我們一起幫助保護我們的環境。我們需要保護地球因為它是我們的家。我們不需要做大不了的事 — 我們可以從小處著手。不要把任何垃圾丟到地上。不要浪費水。當你書寫時使用紙的兩面。停止使用塑膠袋購物。

This is our world. Let's do our best to make it more beautiful.

這是我們的世界。讓我們盡力使它更美麗。

17. The speakers asked three questions at the beginning and the answers to these questions are all "No".(講者在一開始問了三個問題而這些問題的答案都是「不」。)

答案：(T 對)

18. Grandmother often tells the speaker some stories about her childho

(祖母經常講一些關於她童年的故事給講者聽。)

答案：(F 錯)

19. It seems that in the city people lived in a cleaner environment many years ago.

(看樣子在都市的人們多年前住在一個較乾淨的環境。)

答案：(T 對)

20. The speaker told us that people are doing something bad to the city now.

(講者告訴我們人們現在正在對都市做一些有害的事。)

答案：(T 對)

21. The speaker thought that the Earth is in trouble.(講者認為地球正陷入麻煩。)

答案：(T對)

22. The speaker seemed to be a member of an organization which helps protect the environment.

(講者似乎是一個幫助保護環境的組織的成員。)

答案：(T 對)

23. The speaker suggested we reuse plastic bags for shopping.

(講者建議我們重複使用購物塑膠袋。)

答案：(F 錯)

Ⅳ、Listen to the dialogue and fill in the blanks.

Ben: Hi, Angela, I am writing an article, "How do you feel about these problems?", for our school newspaper. Can you give me a hand?

(班：嗨，安吉拉，我正在為我們的校刊寫一篇文章，「你對這些問題感覺如何？」

妳可以幫我個忙嗎？）

Angela: No problem. (安吉拉：沒問題。)

Ben: First, I will tell you about a problem. Then I will ask you, "How do you feel about it?" There are three choices for your answer: not worried at all, a little worried or very worried. OK? (班：首先，我將告訴妳一個問題。然後我會問妳，妳對此感覺如何？妳有三個選項可以回答：完全不擔憂，有點擔憂，或是很擔憂。好嗎？)

Angela: OK. (安吉拉：好。)

Ben: Here's the first problem: People throwing rubbish in parks, streets and other places. How do you feel about it? (班：這是第一個問題：人們在公園街到和其他地方丟垃圾。妳對此感覺如何？)

Angela: Oh, those people don't care about the environment or about other people. That's so bad. My answer is "very worried". (安吉拉：噢，這些人不在乎環境或其他人。真糟糕。我的答案是「很擔憂」。)

Ben: Now, the second one: People making a lot of noise. (班：現在，第二個：人們製造很多噪音。)

Angela: I'm not worried about this. We can put something over our ears. My answer is "not worried at all".(安吉拉：我不為此擔憂。我們可以用某種東西蓋住耳朵。我的答案是「完全不擔憂」。)

Ben: Got it. Now, the third one: People polluting the water and the air.
(班：明白了。現在，第三個：人們污染水和空氣。)

Angela: Well, no one can live without water or air. My answer is "very worried".
(安吉拉：嗯，沒有人可以在沒有水或空氣之下生活。我的答案是「很擔憂」。)

Ben: That's what I think too. The last problem: A lot of traffic on the road.
(班：我也是那樣想。最後一個問題：道路交通擁擠。)

Angela: Well, my answer is "a little worried". (安吉拉：嗯，我的答案是「有點擔憂」。)

Ben: Well, that's all. Thanks a lot. (班：好，就這些。多謝了。)

Angela: My pleasure. (安吉拉：我很樂意。)

QUESTIONNAIRE: How do you feel about these __24__?
(問卷：你對這些問題有什麼感覺？)

Your choices: (你的選項)

A＞not worried at all 完全不擔憂

B＞a __25__ worried 有點擔憂

C＞very worried 很擔憂

Question 1: People throwing __26__ in parks, streets and __27__ places.
(問題一：人們在公園街到和其他地方丟垃圾。)

Question 2: People making a lot of __28__. (問題二：人們製造很多噪音。)

Question 3: People __29__ the water and the air. (問題三：人們污染水和空氣。)

Question 4: A lot of __30__ on the road. (問題四：道路交通擁擠。)

24. 答案：problems
25. 答案：little
26. 答案：rubbish
27. 答案：other
28. 答案：noise
29. 答案：polluting
30. 答案：traffic

Unit 15

I、Listen and choose the right picture.（根據你所聽到的內容，選出相應的圖片）（5分）

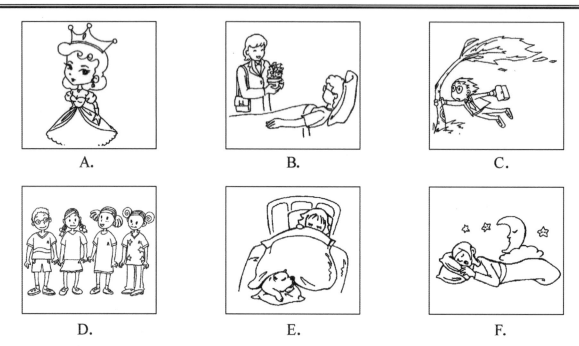

A.　　　　　　　B.　　　　　　　C.

D.　　　　　　　E.　　　　　　　F.

1. Kitty hopes she will be as good-looking as the beauty in the future.
   （Kitty 希望將來她會像美女一樣漂亮。）

   答案：(A)

2. The terrible wind nearly blows Tom away!
   （可怕的風幾乎要把 Tom 吹走了。）

   答案：(C)

3. Do you feel better now, John? These flowers are for you.
   （John，你現在覺得好一些嗎？這些花是給你的。）

   答案：(B)

4. The four children hope they will be friends forever.
   （四個孩子希望他們永遠都是好朋友。）

   答案：(D)

5. The puppy jumped onto the bed at midnight and slept together with the little girl.
   （那隻小狗在午夜跳上床和小女孩一起睡。）

   答案：(E)

6. I think Jacky will be a smart boy in the future.
   （我認為 Jacky 將來會是一個聰明的男孩。）
   (A)smell（聞）   (B)smile（笑）
   (C)small（小的）   (D)smart（聰明的）
   答案：(D)

7. Read the note on the back and you will know what you will be like in 20 years' time.
   （讀一讀背後的記錄，你就會知道二十年後你會像甚麼。）
   (A)night（晚上）   (B)nice（很好）
   (C)note（記錄）   (D)nose（鼻子）
   答案：(C)

8. The photo on the front shows how you will look in 20 years' time.
   （正面的照片告訴你二十年後你會長得如何。）
   (A)from（從…）   (B)front（前面）
   (C)frog（青蛙）   (D)fog（霧）
   答案：(B)

9. Route C takes the shortest time.
   （路線 C 花最少的時間。）
   (A)road（道路）   (B)read（讀）
   (C)rope（繩子）   (D)route（路線）
   答案：(D)

10. Would you like to be a baker in the future?
    （你將來想成為一位烘焙師嘛？）
    (A)bake（烘焙）   (B)back（背後）
    (C)baker（烘焙師）   (D)bad（壞的）
    答案：(C)

III、**Listen and choose the best response to the sentence you hear.** （根據你所聽到的句子，選出最恰當的應答句。）（5分）

11. When does your first class begin?（你第一堂課甚麼時候開始？）
    (A)We have no class.（我們沒有課。）
    (B)I'm in Class One.（我在一班。）

(C)At eight in the morning. （在早上八點。）

(D)In the evening. （在下午。）

答案：(C)

12. What time is it now?（現在幾點？）

(A)My watch is slow. （我的錶慢了。）

(B)Yours is ten minutes fast. （你的快了十分鐘。）

(C)Maybe I know. （我或許知道。）

(D)It's five twenty-five. （五點二十五分。）

答案：(D)

13. Where does the bus stop?（公車停在哪裡？）

(A)I don't know the bus stop. （我不知道公車站。）

(B)The bus doesn't stop here. （公車不在這兒停。）

(C)Only cars stop here. （只有汽車停這兒。）

(D)At the next corner. （在下一個轉角。）

答案：(D)

14. What's the date today?（今天幾號？）

(A)It's Sunday. （今天星期天。）

(B)It's September the third. （今天是九月三日。）

(C)It's a hot day. （今天很熱。）

(D)It's our holiday. （今天是我們的節日。）

答案：(B)

15. Would you like a cup of tea?（你想要一杯茶嗎？）

(A)You're welcome. （不客氣。）　　(B)All right. （太好了。）

(C)Yes, please. （好，請給我。）　　(D)No, I needn't. （不，我不需要。）

答案：(C)

IV、Listen to the dialogue and choose the best answer to the question you hear.（根據你所聽到的對話和問題，選出最恰當的答案。）(5分)

16. M: Was it hot last summer?

（M: 去年夏天熱嗎？）

W: Yes. The August was very hot last year.

（W: 熱。去年八月非常熱。）

Question: Which month was very hot last year?

（問題：去年的那一個月份非常熱？）

(A)August.（八月。）

(B)July.（七月。）

(C)June.（六月。）

(D)June and August.（六月和八月。）

答案：(A)

17. M: Hello, Nancy. This is Tom. Is Tim at home?

（M:哈囉，Nancy。我是 Tom。Tim 在家嗎？）

W: He is in class now.

（W: 他現在在上課。）

Question: Who is in class now?

（問題：誰現在在上課？）

(A)Tom.（Tom。）

(B)Tim.（Tim。）

(C)Nancy.（Nancy。）

(D)The boy.（那個男孩。）

答案：(B)

18. M: Were you born in Shanghai?

（M:你在上海生的嗎？）

W: No. I was born in Beijing. I moved here at the age of five.

（W: 不，我生在北京。我五歲的時候搬來這裡。）

Question: Where was the girl born?

（問題：女孩在哪裡出生？）

(A)In Shanghai.（在上海。）

(B)In Nanjing.（在南京。）

(C)In Beijing.（在北京。）

(D)In Tianjin.（在天津。）

答案：(C)

19. M: Can I help you?

（M: 我能幫你嗎？）

W: I want to borrow some story books.

（W: 我想借一些故事書。）

Question: Where does the dialogue take place?

（問題：這段對話在哪裡發生？）

(A)In a shop.（在商店。）

(B)In the library.（在圖書館。）

(C)On the playground.（在遊樂場。）

(D)In the hospital.（在醫院。）

答案：(B)

20. M: Excuse me, could you please tell me the way to the English teachers' office?

　　（M: 不好意思，你能告訴我該怎麼去英語老師的辦公室嗎？）

W: Go upstairs. It's Room 405.

　　（W: 上樓。在 405 號房。）

Question: Where's the English teachers' office?

　　（問題：英語老師的辦公室在哪裡？）

(A)Room 405.（405 號房。）

(B)Room 404.（404 號房。）

(C)Room 504.（504 號房。）

(D)Room 505.（505 號房。）

答案：(A)

Ⅴ、Listen to the passage and decide whether the following statements are True (T) or False (F). （判斷下列句子內容是否符合你所聽到的短文內容，符合的用 T 表示，不符合的用 F 表示。）(5 分)

Alice loves dressing up. (Alice 愛打扮。)

In 10 years' time, Alice will be tall and slim. (十年後，Alice 會變得又高又瘦。)

She will be very good-looking. (她會非常好看。)

She will possibly be 172 centimeters tall and weigh 54 kilograms.

(她大概會有一百七十二公分高， 五十四公斤重。)

She will be good at singing because she likes singing very much.

(因為她非常喜歡唱歌所以她會唱得很好。)

But her mother doesn't want her to be a singer or a model.

(但是她母親不希望她成為歌手或是模特兒。)

She hopes her daughter will study hard and practise English more every day.

(她希望女兒可以每天多努力學習英語。)

And then she can go to a good university. (然後她可以進一所好大學。)

She wants her to be a teacher, a doctor or something like that.

(她希望她當老師、醫生之類的工作。)

21. Alice loves dressing up and she will be very beautiful.
   （Alice 愛打扮而且她會非常漂亮。）
   答案：（T 對）

22. She will possibly be a model or a singer.
   （她可能將成為一位模特兒或是歌手。）
   答案：（T 對）

23. Her mother also wants her to be a model or a singer.
   （她的母親也希望她成為一位模特兒或是歌手。）
   答案：（F 錯）

24. She will be 170 centimeters tall and 54 kilograms heavy.
   （她將有一百七十公分高、五十四公斤重。）
   答案：（F 錯）

25. Alice studies hard and she is good at English.
   （Alice 努力學習並且她英語很棒。）
   答案：（F 錯）

VI、Listen to the dialogue and complete the notes. （根據你所聽到的對話內容，用適當的單詞完成下面的筆記。每空格限填一個單詞。）（5分）

M: Look, Linda! That's the magic camera!
（M: 看，Linda。那是魔術照像機。）

W: What did you say, Jack? A magic camera?
（W: Jack，你說甚麼？魔術照像機？）

M: Yes. It can tell you what you'll possibly be in 20 years' time.
（M: 是的。它能告訴你二十年後你可能會變成甚麼。）

W: Really? That sounds amazing!
（W: 真的嗎？聽起來太神奇了！）

M: Let me try it first.
（M: 讓我先試試看。）

W: Oh, here is the note. What does it say?
（W: 喔，這是記錄。上面說甚麼？）

M: It says: In 20 years' time, I will be 25 centimeters taller. Ha, ha ... Oh, no!
（M: 它說：二十年後，我會比現在高二十五公分。哈哈…喔，不！）

W: What's wrong?
（W: 怎麼了？）

M: It says I will be 30 kilograms heavier. But now I only weigh 50 kilograms.
（M: 它說我將會比現在重三十公斤。但是我現在只有五十公斤重。）

W: You must make your diet better now, or you will be too heavy. What else does it say?
（W: 你現在必須要注意飲食，要不然你會太重。它還說些甚麼？）

M: It also says that I will be strong and will be good at cooking.
（M: 它也說我會很強壯而且很會煮菜。）

W: Cooking? I quite agree because you enjoy eating very much.
（W: 煮菜？我還蠻同意的因為你非常享受吃東西。）

M: It says I will possibly be a teacher. But I really want to be a cook.
（M: 它說我可能會當老師。但是我好想當廚師。）

W: That's funny. Now let me have a try.
（W: 真有趣。現在讓我試試。）

- Jack will be __26__ centimetres taller.
  （Jack 將會更高＿＿＿公分。）

- Jack will weigh __27__ kilograms.
  （Jack 將有＿＿＿公斤重。）

- Jack will be __28__.
  （Jack 將會＿＿＿。）

- Jack will be good at __29__.
  （Jack 將會擅長於＿＿＿。）

- Jack will probably be a__30__.
  （Jack 可能會當＿＿＿。）

26. 答案：25 (二十五)

27. 答案：80 (八十)

28. 答案：strong (強壯的)

29. 答案：cooking (煮菜/料理)

30. 答案：teacher (老師)

全新國中會考英語聽力精選【中】

出版者：夏朵文理補習班

出版發行：禾耘圖書文化有限公司

地址：新北市新店區安祥路109巷15號

電話：02-29422385　傳真：02-29426087

劃撥帳號：50231111禾耘圖書文化有限公司

總經銷：紅螞蟻圖書有限公司

地址：台北市114內湖區舊宗路2段121巷28號4樓

網站：www.e-redant.com

電話：02-27953656　傳真：02-27954100

劃撥帳號：16046211紅螞蟻圖書有限公司

ISBN：978-986-94976-1-9　（中冊：平裝）

出版日期:106年6月

本書由華東師範大學出版社有限公司授權
夏朵文理補習班出版發行

定價400元